BILL MATTHEWS lived and worked in Turkey, Italy and Canada before moving to Cambridge, England where he built his business career before joining the University of Cambridge to run the university's seed fund investing in start-up companies.

Since giving up full time work, he has written short stories, family histories and his first novel *The Venetian*. He is working now on a second novel and a book of short stories

C000000024

THE
VENETIAN

Bill Matthews

SilverWood

Published in 2021 by SilverWood Books

SilverWood Books Ltd
14 Small Street, Bristol, BS1 1DE, United Kingdom
www.silverwoodbooks.co.uk

ISBN 978-1-80042-064-9 (paperback)
ISBN 978-1-80042-065-6 (ebook)

British Library Cataloguing in Publication Data
A CIP catalogue record for this book is
available from the British Library

Page design and typesetting by SilverWood Books

To my wife, Bridget, our children and grandchildren

Contents

Foreword	Arriving in Istanbul	9
1	Preparing to Leave Venice	13
2	Voyage to Constantinople	25
3	Letters of Introduction	39
4	Throat Cutter on the Bosphorus	53
5	Mehmed Plans the Siege	65
6	Constantine Seeks Help	75
7	The Siege Begins	85
8	Pounding of the Walls	101
9	Encircled by Fire	111
10	Fall of Constantinople	121
11	Flight from the City	129
12	Vengeance is Mine	135
13	Return to Venice	141
14	Reporting to Council	149
15	Lunch with George Sphrantzes	159
16	I Nozze di Nicolò	167
17	Setting up a Practice	181
18	The Conqueror Advances	189
19	George Enters a Monastery	199
20	The Plague Ship	203
21	Moving Forward	219
Afterword	Farewell to Istanbul	225
	Bibliography	229

Foreword

Arriving in Istanbul
February 1964

I was looking out of the window of the Comet 4 airliner searching for the lights of a city below. I had never been to Istanbul, which made me excited and, at the same time, more than a little apprehensive. At the age of twenty-four it was to be my first job.

Tony Newbery, the senior partner, had interviewed me in London. He was a charming man of the old school and was recruiting an audit manager; that is, someone with considerably more experience than myself, but, as luck would have it, Tony knew my father's cousin, Sybil Hambidge, who was assistant to the naval attaché at the British Consulate. The interview became a matter of whom I knew rather than what I knew. He offered me the job.

The Comet's flight path brought it in over the sea, its wing lights reflecting up from the water. As the plane continued its sharp descent, it almost looked as if we might land in the water, but then the plane took a final, stomach-churning plunge down. *Bang! Bang!* The wheels made contact with the runway. We bounced three times before slowing, braking, and coming to a halt. The plane turned left onto a taxiway and rumbled gently towards a down-at-heel building with a glass front.

We disembarked and walked across the tarmac. Compared to Heathrow it all looked very third world and reminded me of the terminal in the film *Casablanca*. Above the entrance was a neon sign: Yeşilköy Airport. The passengers crowded into the customs and baggage area. It was hot and stuffy. The Turkish customs officer, a large man sweating profusely above his bushy black moustache, gave my passport a cursory glance before stamping it fiercely. My new life had begun.

I was driven from the airport into Istanbul by Tony Newbery and Jo, his secretary. It was a Sunday and Tony Newbery was dressed in a suit and tie as if for the office. I noticed that they looked a little surprised to see me, but Tony was far too courteous to point out that I had arrived a day early. I sat in the back of the leather-upholstered Humber looking out into the night as we passed through Bakirköy. We drove along the coast road. It was crowded with old American Prohibition-era cars which served in those days as taxis in Istanbul. On the seashore, to my right, were lines of restaurants. Dark-skinned men in black suits and flat caps sat around the tables eating, drinking and playing cards. There were no women. Strings of weak, coloured light bulbs were suspended from electric cables above the tables.

After about an hour, we were approaching the city through the village of Zeytinburnu. Here the road passed under the arch of a Roman aqueduct. I could see that the huge stone structure stretched away on the left into the darkening countryside. We were travelling parallel to the old city walls. In places they had been blasted away leaving gaps through which a man could pass into the inner city. The people living among the ruins looked like gypsies, and around them ran children in tattered clothes. Families had constructed primitive shelters high up in the walls to be safe from intruders. Every here and there fires had been lit in front of the shacks. Supper was being prepared.

Fifty-five years have passed since that evening. I have written this book which is set in the city of Constantinople at the time of the fall of the Byzantine Empire in 1453. The book is based on historical events but is written as a novel rather than a history. It draws, in part, on the eyewitness account of the events written in the diary of a young Venetian doctor, Nicolò Barbaro, in the final days of the Byzantine Empire. The story begins with his leaving Venice, continues with his adventures in Constantinople and the Aegean, and ends with his final return to Venice on board a ship infected with the plague. The book is based on historical events and actual people who existed at the time. But it is also a novel so imagines the feelings, the words and lives of the characters as if it were a drama. Hopefully, readers will be able to accept this mixture of historical fact and the author's imagination in the spirit intended, that is, to tell an exciting story.

The surprising thing, I find, is how little the city of Istanbul has changed since 1453. You can walk down the same roads and climb the same walls which bear the marks of the Ottoman bombardment. The Turks, the Greeks, the Italians, the Armenians and the Jews are living in the same districts. The foreign consulates are still in the Pera. From my office in Beyoğlu, I can look down onto the harbour where the Turkish fleet lay at anchor during the siege.

Bill Matthews

1

Preparing to Leave Venice
1451

It was early morning in Venice in the year of Our Lord 1451. A mist was rising from the lagoon, drifting across the peeling paint of the palazzi lining the Grand Canal, curling around the cupolas of churches and spreading its thin, insubstantial veil over the shipyards. The young man standing on the Rialto Bridge was waiting for something dramatic to happen. Then, as if a stagehand had drawn back a curtain, the rising sun evaporated the moisture in the air and revealed to him the city of Venice – La Serenissima. Below, a ferry was crossing the Grand Canal crowded with housewives and their servants on their way to market. The morning air was heavy with the delicious smell of newly baked bread. Overhead the seabirds wheeled, screeching and diving. The tidal waters gurgled and splashed their way around the foundations of the ancient buildings, releasing an odour of damp and rotting timber. It was the smell of Venice. He breathed in the mixture of decay, fresh bread, market stalls, vegetables, fish, pungent cheeses and dried herbs. The smell excited, as it always did, every human sense.

Dr Nicolò Barbaro was the young man standing on the bridge. He was the youngest son of a Venetian patrician family. From where he stood he could see the family palazzo, consisting of an imposing residence, a warehouse, and a landing stage fronting onto the Grand Canal. His family made their living as traders and his father had urged him to join the family business, but Nicolò did not want to spend his life buying and selling dried fruits, spices and cloth, even if it would make him rich. He had chosen instead to study medicine at Padua University which was a world leader in medical research. It had been a very stimulating and challenging course. Now his studies were complete and Nicolò had returned to Venice after graduating in May 1451. He knew that, after many years of study, he wanted to escape from this claustrophobic city of narrow alleys and secretive whispers. He did not want to live his life as his parents had lived theirs, as prosperous but dull burghers. Also, he had become bored with his student friends and their evenings of drinking and loose women. He felt that he had progressed beyond such adolescent pastimes. His first thought had been to set up his own practice in Venice, but he did not have enough money nor the practical experience. He felt restless and realised that this might be the only time in his life, before he settled down, when he could explore the exciting and dangerous world which lay beyond the Venetian lagoon.

But he had encountered a problem. His mother wanted him to get married. His mother's friends had suggested to her that Nicolò, now twenty-five years of age, needed a wife. Their advice was not entirely disinterested. They had daughters to settle and here was a handsome young man of good family with excellent prospects. They pressed the case for their daughters as strongly as they could without seeming too anxious. But, of course, they were anxious. Unmarried daughters were expensive with an unlimited demand for new gowns and tickets to society balls. They hung around the family palazzo looking unhappy and discontented. The sooner they got married the better.

Nicolò's mother had asked him to visit her boudoir a few days before, for a chat. She was a fine woman of middle years with dark hair gathered elegantly at the back of her head. Her velvet dress was cut low at the front, allowing visitors a discreet glimpse of her full bosom, and she wore a necklace of black semi-precious stones around her neck. His mother had reached an age when she had become dedicated to organising and managing her family. She had arranged satisfactory marriages for his two older sisters and now she must get Nicolò settled. She looked at him fondly across the oak table. Without doubt, even allowing for a mother's bias, her son was a most attractive young man. His face had a sculptured look with prominent cheekbones, firm nose and chin. His eyes were the blue of the sea, and he had an open and direct gaze full of intelligence. Perhaps he was a little conceited and self-centred, but then most young men suffer from those faults. Fortunately, his mother reflected, he had not inherited his father's dark complexion which was fine for a businessman trading in the

Orient but not for a consultant in the medical profession. She was inordinately proud of her son and wanted the best for him, so had compiled a shortlist of marriageable young women who might be suitable.

She said in her softest and most persuasive voice, 'Caro, your father and I think it is time for you to settle down. You have completed your studies and need to establish your own medical practice. People trust doctors who are married. A wife could help you with running the practice and promote it to her friends. She would also bring a dowry which would be most helpful. I should like to introduce you to some young ladies, any of whom would make you an excellent wife.'

'Mother, I don't want to meet any young ladies,' Nicolò interjected, 'and I don't want to get married. I have more important things to do.'

His mother could not imagine what could be more important than getting married. Frankly, she was a little shocked at his brusque rejection of her proposal. However, if her son refused to meet these young women there was little prospect of concluding a marriage agreement. She decided to be patient. She had planted the idea in his mind where it would mature in good time. In her experience young men eventually came around to appreciating the benefits of having a beautiful young wife to warm their marital bed.

Later, talking to her husband, she said, 'Let him get it out of his system, this travelling business. When he returns, he will be ready to settle down – just leave it to me.'

Her husband agreed. Arranging marriages was a task best left to his wife. At least in this case he would not have to provide a dowry as he had for his daughters, which had left him poorer.

Of course, in the longer term, such alliances might be good investments, but in the short term they did nothing to improve cash flow. So his parents agreed between them that the sooner Nicolò set off on his travels the sooner he would return. Then he could marry. Perhaps it was for the best.

His father arranged for him to meet Francesco Foscari, the Doge of Venice, to get his advice and approval of Nicolò's travel plans. The meeting with the Doge was to be that July morning so he walked down the Rialto Bridge, entered a passage which led around a corner, then up and over a narrow stone bridge. There was a line of gondolas moored underneath the bridge where the morning sun had not penetrated. The water looked cold and black. A little further on and the street took him out into the sunlit Piazza San Marco. At the far end of the piazza stood the Church of San Marco in all its Byzantine splendour.

He walked across the pavement to the Doge's palace and hurried up the long flight of stairs. An attendant showed him into the room where Foscari sat at an oak table. Sunlight flickered through the shutters behind the seated figure. His face was in shadow, perhaps by design, to disconcert visitors. He stood up to welcome Nicolò. He was old, his skin sallow and the jowls slack. A heavy embroidered cloak covered his shoulders and he wore a velvet cap, lined with fur, on his head. Here was an old man worn out by his responsibilities. He wasted no time on pleasantries.

'Dottore Barbaro, congratulations on your excellent results at Padua and on becoming a doctor. Your father is justly proud of your achievements. He tells me that you wish to travel and are set on going to Constantinople.'

'Yes, Excellency, that is my intention.'

The Doge continued, 'I quite understand your wish to travel, young man. I was the same when I was your age and I should like to help if you will permit. By coincidence I have been asked to appoint a medical officer to the town of Galata, which is close to Constantinople. It occurred to me that you might be just the man for the job. Your patients would be merchants, their families and the crews of visiting ships. It would be a good place to practise your new medical skills – put the theory into practice, so to speak, without doing too much damage. You would be paid a salary and reimbursed for your living and travel expenses. After an agreed term, if you had done well, you could return and set up a practice here in Venice. We might even persuade you to get married.'

Nicolò felt annoyed that his father must have mentioned his getting married. But the offer of employment in Constantinople was too good to turn down. He accepted then and there.

'Good.' The Doge continued, 'My secretary will make the necessary arrangements of travel permits, letters of introduction, bills of exchange and accommodation in Galata and so on. With your permission my secretary will book your passage for early September.'

Nicolò agreed, perhaps a little too eagerly.

'Now,' said the Doge, 'there is another matter you could help me with. We live in volatile and dangerous times. The Byzantine Emperor, Constantine, has appealed to Venice for help. The Emperor needs money, soldiers and food to defend the city against the Ottoman Turks. Constantine has travelled around Europe with his begging bowl. Western nations are reluctant to help him, not least because the Byzantine Emperor has cried wolf once too often. The Pope will help only on condition that the schism between the Orthodox and Roman churches is satisfactorily resolved. In any case, the consensus among western allies is that Sultan Mehmed, who is still very young and inexperienced, will not dare to attack Constantinople. The Council of Ten has turned down Constantine's request, but I fear that it may have been wrong to do so. They believe that God is on the side of the Christians, though I am not sure that God has a side, but if he has, history suggests that it is the side with the most money and the largest army. I am convinced that the Turks pose a serious threat to Christian Europe. Their armies surround Constantinople, control the Dardanelles, and they have occupied European Thrace. They can draw on fresh troops from the Asian steppes whenever they need them, and they have the men, money and other resources to take Constantinople and then press on down through the Balkans and Hungary and even attack Vienna.'

'In what way can I help, Excellency? I am a doctor not a military man.'

'I want you to be my eyes and ears in Constantinople. With better intelligence we can frustrate the Sultan's plans and support the Emperor, provided we don't start a war or damage our trading relations with the Ottomans. I need someone on the spot who will report to me personally. Would you be prepared to help me?'

'Of course, Excellency. I should be honoured.'

The Doge looked across at Nicolò. The young man's face was unlined and betrayed no signs of misfortune or adversity. Perhaps he was too naive and weak to be an effective spy. Was he just a cosseted mother's boy like so many young men in Venice? On the other hand, there was no one else he could send. As Doge of Venice he had to use people in the interests of the state, even if that meant putting them in harm's way. The interests of Venice always took precedence as far as he was concerned.

'I must warn you that this could be dangerous. No one must know you are working for me – not even your father. The Turks have short and brutal ways of dealing with spies.'

It was only when he was walking back across St Mark's Square that Nicolò realised how skilfully the Doge had played him. Perhaps it had been planned in advance with his father's approval. Or was it his own vanity that had been his undoing, and the enticing prospect of dangerous and romantic adventure? But again, he had been asked to report to the Doge personally on issues of national importance. It was heady stuff for a young man. How could he refuse? It was a relief to get away from the gloom of the Doge's palace and to be in the piazza, where the warmth of the sun dispelled his fears and doubts. The gondoliers were shouting, their boats were grinding against the mooring posts and the passengers were haggling about fares in raised voices. It was all so reassuringly normal.

He prepared to leave Venice in September. His father suggested that he take Bartoletti with him as a companion and bodyguard. Bartoletti was a former centurion in the Hungarian army. He had been captured ten years earlier during the war between Venice and Milan. Nicolò's father had bought him in the Venetian slave market. The ex-soldier had proved to be trustworthy and intelligent, so much so that he had been promoted to the position of steward. Bartoletti was a tall man with strong broad shoulders. His beard was white and neatly trimmed, while his head was balding at the back. He looked every inch a soldier, and with his steady gaze he was a reassuring presence. Other staff looked up to him. He never talked of his life before he became a slave. Did he have a wife and children in Hungary? No one knew and he never volunteered any information. He was a man who could keep his own counsel. Nicolò's father promised Bartoletti privately that he would grant him his freedom if he brought his son safely home.

The day before their departure, in the family palazzo, the two men set about packing for their voyage. 'There are two very important things,' Nicolò explained. 'First are my medical instruments. These are delicate and I shall need to check each item, and second, we will need armour and weapons in case we have to defend ourselves. You are the military man, Bartoletti, so you must decide what we need to take.'

'I have already prepared a list, sir.' Bartoletti pointed to the table where he had laid out a selection of armour and weapons. 'The clothes and equipment are in the order in which we will put them on. First are woollen undergarments which are padded in front and belted at the waist to give comfort and warmth. Then we put on this long, thick shirt, which will absorb some of the impact of enemy blows. Over that you put on this long cuirass, then these tassets cover the thighs, and this codpiece is for your future wife's peace of mind! For the head there are these Venetian helmets. Lastly, there are thick leather gloves and a small round shield. Our weapons include these swords and daggers.' Bartoletti caressed the blades glinting in the light of the window. 'I will sharpen these before we leave.'

Nicolò was impressed. 'Bartoletti, this is an excellent selection, but hopefully they will not be needed. If the worst comes to the worst, we can take the next ship home.'

Later, he was to reflect on these words. How naive he had been to plan an escape while others continued fighting. Could they run for home leaving friends and patients to their fate? He thought not. He was convinced that he would never turn his back on the enemy.

A carpenter had built a wooden chest to carry the medical items. The upper section of the chest was for medicines and the lower section for surgical instruments and dressings. In addition, within the chest, there was a drawer for ointments and salves. The instruments included scissors, forceps, spatulas, grooved dissectors, cannulas, clamps, retractors, knives, needles, saws, artery clips, screw tourniquets and catheters, and all that was needed to treat wounds and injuries. They packed and boxed the medical instruments, armour and weapons, and other necessities for the voyage to Constantinople.

Equally important were the Doge's letters of introduction, paper, and invisible ink for writing his reports. The letters included were addressed to the Emperor Constantine, to George Sphrantzes, the Greek historian, to Girolamo Minotto, the Venetian bailor, to Halil Pasha, the Sultan's Grand Vizier, who was known to be sympathetic to the Byzantine cause, and to Loukas Notares, Constantine's Grand Admiral, and, finally, a letter of introduction to the supervisor of the Port of Gallipoli.

The following day the porters took the baggage down to their ship. All that remained was to say farewell to family and friends and to take a gondola to the ship early the next morning. Nicolò's parents were determined to give their son a good send-off, and they invited family, friends and business partners to attend. All entertaining at their palazzo provided an opportunity to promote his father's business and tonight was no exception. Everything was in good taste with fine wines and excellent food. The ladies wore their best gowns and held masks in front of their dark eyes to add mystery and allure. Musicians played antique stringed instruments. The guests took their leave after Nicolò and Bartoletti finally departed.

It was dawn on the tenth of September 1451. A household servant helped carry their hand luggage to the pontoon, where they stood together in the chilly air waiting for a gondola to take them to the shipyard. Bartoletti shouted across to a gondolier huddled asleep under a covering of blankets at the nearby mooring post. The man awoke with a start. In a moment, the boat was making its way across the canal. After loading their belongings, they stepped on board. The gondolier leaned his weight against the oar, and the gondola glided away from the pontoon. They were on their way.

2

Voyage to Constantinople
September–November 1451

A t the dockyard they boarded the *San Marco*, an armed merchant galley. Two other ships, also built in Venice, the *San Pietro* and the *San Paulo*, were tied up further down the dock. All three ships were of similar design, with raised defensive platforms fore and aft, twin masts with furled lateen sails and crow's nests for lookouts and the crossbow archers. A number of soldiers were already on board, busily stowing armour and weapons. The archers hung their shields along the ships' rails as protection against enemy arrows and crossbow bolts. The ships were bustling with activity in preparation for sailing on the next tide.

Captain Risso was master of the *San Marco*. He was an experienced adventurer who had sailed merchant galleys in the Mediterranean for many years, but he looked much younger than his forty years. He had a tanned complexion and everything he did was done energetically and with clear purpose. No one could describe Captain Risso as handsome, but he had an open and friendly face and was reputed to have wives and children living in Constantinople and in a number of Mediterranean ports. His head was covered with a blue scarf and he carried a short sword in his waistband. He had a reputation for daring and for taking risks which endeared him to his crew.

He explained to Nicolò, 'Our ships will travel in convoy. Three armed merchantmen together are a tough proposition for pirates or enemy warships.'

'Are attacks likely?' asked Nicolò.

'There are islands along the Adriatic coasts which make good hiding places for pirate ships. Fortunately we have Venetian forts along the coast, and if necessary we can take refuge under the protection of their guns. But, since you ask, attacks are indeed likely. No doubt you have seen action before?'

Nicolò was non-committal. He had not been in action before and could hardly pretend to have been. He hoped that he would not show cowardice in front of these hard men. He recalled the words of Odysseus: "Cowards, I know, would quit the fighting, but the man who wants to make his mark in war must stand his ground." Of course, Nicolò was a doctor and his job was to patch up the wounded not to make his mark in the fighting.

The crews rowed the galleys across the tranquil waters of the lagoon, past the Island of Murano and the Lido, before exiting the lagoon and entering the Gulf of Venice and the Adriatic.

As evening fell, Nicolò could still see in the distance the dome of the San Marco Basilica and the top of the Campanile. The church bells which sounded each hour were growing fainter as the distance increased.

'When will I see Venice again?' he asked himself.

The *San Marco* rose and fell on the sea swell. A north-easterly wind filled the canvas. The rowers noisily shipped their oars and relaxed on their wooden benches. Seabirds kept them company until they were well out to sea. That evening they anchored at Pola on the Istrian Peninsula. Supper was fish grilled over a charcoal fire on the beach and eaten with fresh bread dipped in olive oil. The officers, crew and passengers went ashore to enjoy the feast. There was no deference paid to rank or to worldly status on board a merchant galley. All the crew shared the hazards and dangers of the voyages as well as the rewards. Time would tell who would prove to be brave, who cowardly, who could be trusted in a crisis. On that first night they enjoyed a cheerful meal, drank too much wine and sang songs. As the moon set, the men either drifted away to sleep on the ships, or wrapped themselves in their cloaks and fell asleep on the beach to the sound of the breaking surf, which is what Nicolò and Bartoletti chose to do. Soldiers were posted in the crow's nests to watch for enemy attack. Heaven help them if they fell asleep. The threat of a flogging helped to keep them awake. The watch called out the passing hours, 'Third hour and all's well', until the break of dawn.

The next day the convoy set off up the Adriatic coast. The captain ordered the crew to be on maximum alert as this area was favoured by pirates who hid among the islands like spiders waiting to drop onto unsuspecting flies. Nicolò hoped that the captain's stories of pirates were exaggerated. But no, about ten o'clock there was a cry from the main mast: 'Sails in the north-east – about three miles.' 'How many?' asked Captain Risso. 'Five or six light galleys.' Five minutes later the watch confirmed, 'Pirate ships setting course to intercept.'

Nicolò stood on the aft platform and followed the pirate attack as it unfolded.

The captain shouted, 'Run up the Venetian flag – clear away the bow cannon. Bring up the powder, shot and tinder, break out the weapons and stack them on deck. Issue arrows and crossbow bolts.'

The soldiers and crew were well trained and had faced pirate attacks before. Within half an hour the cannon was primed, arms distributed and armour donned. Then a silence fell over the ship, with only the swish of the bow wave, the tense wind in the rigging and the creaking of timbers audible.

'They will be on us within the hour,' Captain Risso predicted. 'Are you ready, doctor?'

Below, the crew had constructed a makeshift operating theatre to which wounded would be taken. The operating table was a crude construction of wooden planks. The medical chest was placed within reach of the surgeon.

'Yes, captain, I am prepared. Bartoletti will assist me and protect the hospital in case of attack. Please assign two of your crew to carry the wounded down to us.'

'Of course, doctor,' replied the captain. 'We are most fortunate to have you with us.'

Bartoletti had put on his armour and strapped on his weapons. He positioned himself by the entrance to the operating theatre, from which he had a good view of the deck. Nicolò put on only light protection. He would entrust himself to Bartoletti if the pirates managed to get on board.

The convoy moved into a close crescent formation. This was a standard manoeuvre to prevent attackers getting alongside and isolating individual galleys. The pirates were closing fast in their light skiffs which were driven forward by banks of oars. They launched their attack with volleys of arrows at a distance of about four hundred metres. The three Venetian galleys returned fire with cannon and crossbow bolts and arrows fired from the crow's nests. The *San Marco* scored a direct hit on one of the pirate boats which began to take on water. The pirates sustained further damage as the Venetians dropped heavy stones, splintering their decking and crushing fragile skulls. The pirates cast grappling irons upwards to latch onto the ship's rail. Most irons failed to secure a hold and fell back into the sea. If a line caught, the pirates immediately started to climb up, shouting, swearing and wielding their swords. Clad in dirty turbans, torn tunics and trousers cut short at the knee, they were an ill-disciplined rabble and no match for the Venetian sailors. A few made it to the deck but the crew was ready for them. One pirate, bolder and more courageous than the rest, gained the deck and charged towards Bartoletti. The old soldier was ready for him. He parried the pirate's wild blows with his shield, then, as the man's scimitar swept above his head, he thrust his short Roman sword into the man's stomach twisting its blade up into the pirate's rib cage. The man was dead before he collapsed with a groan onto the deck. The body was dragged away by the crew and tossed overboard leaving a smear of blood on the deck. Having repelled the initial wave of attackers, the Venetians poured Greek fire onto their heads. Many were horribly burned and threw themselves into the sea to quench the flames. After a battle lasting an hour, the pirate ships admitted defeat and broke off the action, seeking refuge among the islands.

Only one wounded Venetian sailor had been carried down to the operating theatre. An arrow had gone through his left forearm with the arrowhead extending five inches beyond the arm. It was a serious and painful wound. The assistants laid him on the operating table. The man was moaning, his eyes fixed on the arrowhead protruding from his arm as if he was surprised to see it there.

'What will you do, dottore?' asked Bartoletti.

Nicolò examined the wound. He felt nauseous, but he knew that it was his job to extract the arrow, and that doing so would cause the patient great pain. What he had not explained to Bartoletti and Captain Risso was that he had little practical experience of performing surgery. At medical school they had been permitted to dissect the dead corpses of monkeys and perform autopsies on dead bodies but had not operated on living patients. In other words, this would be his first operation.

Nicolò replied in what he hoped was a confident and professional voice, 'First we put a tourniquet around the upper arm to stem the blood. We will cut off the arrowhead. Then we can draw out the shaft of the arrow, suture the wound to close it up, and apply salves, dressings and bandages.'

He ordered Bartoletti to give the patient a herbal potion to ease the pain. The assistants held the man's arm firmly as Nicolò tightened the tourniquet. The blood flow slowed. Bartoletti held the shaft in both hands while an assistant cut off the arrowhead. Bartoletti held the patient's arm firmly as Nicolò pulled the arrow out through the elbow joint. The patient screamed in agony. They could do little to alleviate the pain other than to work as quickly as possible. Once the arrow was out, Barbaro pulled the flaps of skin together and sutured the wound to close up the hole. He applied herbal salves to the wound and covered it with bandages. The operation had taken about ten minutes.

It was over. Nicolò crossed the deck to the nearest gun port. He retched into the sea, after which he felt less nauseous but was ashamed at betraying such weakness in front of the others. He returned to his patient. The man was pathetically grateful to him.

'Rest now, my friend. You will feel much better in a day or two.'

'Well done, master,' said Bartoletti. 'You saved his arm.'

They emerged on deck just in time to see the last of the pirate ships disappearing among the islands. The convoy resumed its course up the Adriatic. There were to be no further pirate attacks and no wounded on the other boats. The captain put this down to the convoy's fierce resistance. As Captain Risso commented later: 'These thieves want to get rich, but they don't want to fight!'

Two weeks later they entered the Strait of Otranto and made for Corfu, where they took on provisions and restocked armaments. In Corfu's harbour, below the castle, they were safe from attack. Passengers and crew relaxed.

The wounded man began to show worrying signs of infection. He was feverish and his brow hot to the touch; the area around the wound was red and had begun to turn black. An unpleasant smell was evidence of gangrene. Nicolò knew he must operate again if the man was to be saved. This he dreaded because it meant amputating the sailor's arm above the elbow joint. He hesitated to do so due to his lack of experience and the undoubted suffering it would cause the patient, but there was no choice.

31

They scrubbed down the operating theatre again. They laid the patient on the table with a support behind his back to hold his upper body upright. An assistant held his shoulders and upper arms to prevent him from moving his injured arm. The patient was given the herbal drink containing a mild anaesthetic. He crossed himself repeatedly and offered up his sufferings to God, then stretched out his left arm for amputation.

Nicolò must not show weakness. He had laid out his instruments in the order in which they would be needed. He tied a ligature around the man's upper arm, then took up the razor-sharp scalpel and cut deep into the arm. The patient screamed. The dottore ignored him. He located the arteries and veins of the upper arm and tied a ligature round them. The arm muscles he stretched outwards before cutting them, leaving enough muscle to reattach after amputation. The arm bone was exposed. He took the saw in his right hand. Bartoletti held the man's arm horizontally in an unyielding grip. Nicolò sawed through the exposed bone as quickly as he could. He threw the detached section of lower arm into a bucket, then filed down the edges of bone and folded the skin and muscle flaps over the stump. The wound he cauterised with a hot iron. The smell of burning flesh filled the operating theatre. Mercifully, the patient had passed out. Nicolò sutured the wound, applied medicinal salve and then bandaged the stump. The operation was completed in seven minutes. He was improving it seemed. The assistants carried the man out onto the deck, where his fellow crew stood silently looking at their friend to see if he was still alive. There had been a subdued muttering from them when they heard the man screaming during the operation, and they stood aside as he was stretchered away.

Captain Risso said, 'Thank you, doctor, on behalf of us all.'

They sailed the next day into the Ionian Sea. The gloomy mountains of Albania gave way to the low plains along the shores of Greece itself. They sheltered at night among the sandy coves of Levkas, Cephalonia and Zante. Everybody's spirits rose as they sailed among the islands. The snow-capped Pindos Mountains rose in the distance. Although they saw other craft, these were fishing boats and friendly Venetian and Greek traders. They saw no Turkish warships and no pirates.

They sailed down the western coast of the Peloponnese. This part of Greece was controlled by the Byzantines – the brothers of the Emperor Constantine. After a week the convoy rounded Cape Malia and headed north-east through the Aegean Sea towards the Dardanelles. They called at the islands of Hydra, Andros and Lemnos. At Imbros, they transferred the patient to a monastery for longer-term care. They were told some time afterwards that, despite the monks' best efforts, the patient had died a month later.

As they approached the Hellespont, Captain Risso gestured towards the Asian shore. 'They say that the city of Troy once stood there.' Nicolò saw in the distance a flat beach which rose out of the sea over the dunes towards a plain stretching into the distance. The land was featureless and uninteresting. It was hard to credit that this was where the heroic Greek ships had lined up along the shore. Nothing remained to bear witness to ten long years of warfare. The warriors and their ships had long since departed. But an image rose in Nicolò's mind of that great multitude of men lined up for battle, and Homer's words came to his mind: 'So with their high thin cries the ghosts flock now'.

They saw a number of Ottoman galleys in the approaches to the Hellespont. The Turkish forts on both sides of the Dardanelles were armed with cannon, and they could see soldiers walking around. The *San Marco* and its two companions kept close to the European shore to avoid the strong currents. The convoy entered the Port of Gallipoli to pay the transit fees demanded by the Turks, and to make a courtesy call on the port's superintendent who agreed to show his friend, Captain Risso, and Nicolò around the shipyards.

As the *San Marco* approached the port, they got a good view of the harbour and were surprised by the number of Turkish warships anchored there. They counted seventy completed galleys and a further thirty warships under construction. The shipyard bore comparison to the Arsenale in Venice. There were separate areas producing different parts and materials such as munitions, rope and rigging, and there were stockpiles of wood gathered from the Thracian countryside. There seemed to be no shortage of skilled workmen. It was altogether a very professional operation designed to produce galleys on a production line system.

Their convoy sailed from Gallipoli into the Sea of Marmara. The wind was favourable, and they made good headway, passing Marmara Island by mid-morning. That evening they anchored in the Gulf of Moudania, and the following day they weighed anchor and headed for the Princes' Islands and Constantinople. By early afternoon they were off the island of Büyükada. They could see its clusters of white houses and pathways leading down to sheltered coves.

They were only a few hours' sailing from Constantinople when Captain Risso saw a ragged white line on the surface of the water by the Asian shore moving towards them. The sky had taken on a strange yellow tinge as if the air was mixed with sand. The air had become heavy and oppressive as when a hot sirocco blasts up from the south. Something abnormal was happening.

'Squall approaching – lower the sails, secure oars, lash cargo. We will have to run before it. Ready about!' Captain Risso shouted.

The *San Marco* executed its change of direction as quickly as it could, but the galley was not a nimble ship. The storm hit before they could complete the manoeuvre. The sea boiled around the ship and a wall of water struck them amidships, threatening to capsize them. The *San Marco* began to take on water. The sailors bailed desperately, crying out, 'God have mercy on us!' Captain Risso shouted, 'Lash yourselves to the rail!' Some of the men were too slow. The waves swept them overboard and they were gone. All three ships were driven away back towards the Gulf of Moudania. The violent squall was moving faster than the ships could run before it and the seas subsided once it had passed over them. By mid-afternoon they were able to resume course. For the crew, the storm had been a warning to stay away from Constantinople. It was a sign to their superstitious minds that God was making ready to abandon the city.

The ships regained the Princes' Islands. Here the water was crystal clear and blissfully calm. The galleys skirted close to the islands, passing a cliff which plunged vertically into the depths. They drew closer to the city. So this was Constantinople – the mythical city which Nicolò had longed to see since he was a boy. What he saw was not quite as he had imagined it.

The city had an elusive quality like a mirage threatening to disappear at any moment. Perhaps it was the effect of seeing it from a distance over water, but the buildings on the hills, the churches, the palaces and the ruins of ancient forums and stadia, and the circle of defensive walls seemed insubstantial and more like an artist's impression than a real place of bricks and stone.

The ships approached closer to the city. Now Nicolò could see houses and even some of the eighty thousand population going about their business. The galleys held a course of about half a mile offshore, heading for the entrance to the Golden Horn. When the ships reached the harbour on the twenty-eighth of October, the oarsmen took their places and rowed the ship across to Galata.

Nicolò and Bartoletti disembarked. To their surprise, a crowd of people were gathered on the dock. There was a short speech of welcome from the Genoese Podestà of Galata. Some people clapped. The Podestà welcomed them with, 'You see, dottore, how pleased everyone is that you have come.' With that, a little procession formed. People helped carry their luggage and the medical instruments. They were escorted through the town gates and up some narrow, vertiginous steps on their still shaky legs to a large wooden house which had been allocated to them. It was here that their medical practice was to be based.

Mary Celovic welcomed them. She was, Nicolò guessed, in her early thirties with dark hair drawn back so as to leave her oval Greek face open and visible for inspection. On her face was the determined expression of an independent woman. She wore an antique gold blouse secured at the throat with a brown silk bow. They were told later that she had inherited the house when her husband, a sea captain, failed to return from a voyage to Odessa. Now she rented out rooms in the house to balance the books. She had received, but rejected, several proposals of marriage, because she was unsure if the suitors wanted her for the house or herself. She did not believe their protestations of love, and in any case she did not need to remarry. So she welcomed the young Venetian surgeon with more genuine enthusiasm than was usual with her tenants, because he was of good family and very handsome. As for Nicolò, he found her attractive and challenging, for she had about her the mysterious allure of an Aegean island set in crystal waters and bathed in sunshine – but this was his first brush with the warmth and beauty of eastern women so no doubt the feeling would pass off soon enough.

Mary had prepared a light supper for them of small grilled fish, fresh bread, fruit and white wine. It was enough to revive their spirits. Under her solicitous care, Nicolò and Bartoletti began to relax, knowing that the rigours of the journey from Venice were at an end. Nicolò slept soundly that night undisturbed by the noises of the crew, the creak of oars and the wind blowing in the sails. On waking, the screech of seabirds outside the window reminded him that they were still close to the sea and that there was much to do.

Nicolò wrote his first report to the Doge that morning. This was encrypted and dispatched on a Venetian ship leaving for Venice.

Report to the Doge:
1 November 1451

Your Excellency,
A few days ago, I visited the Ottoman shipyards at Gallipoli with Captain Risso. We were surprised by the scale and efficiency of the enemy's warship construction programme. The Turks have at least one hundred galleys completed, or nearing completion, at Gallipoli. The addition of one hundred extra war galleys, of which we were unaware, when added to the already substantial Turkish fleet, will challenge Byzantine and Venetian control of the seas. The Turkish shipbuilding effort reinforces the Podestà's

view that Sultan Mehmed intends to attack Constantinople.
An enlarged Turkish fleet could be used to block supply routes
through the Dardanelles and make it difficult for allies to get aid
to Emperor Constantine. On this evidence, Constantine's plea
for help is justified. The Turkish threat is real enough.

Your respectful servant
Dot. Nicolò Barbaro

3

Letters of Introduction
November 1451

 icolò burrowed under the bed covers to harvest a little of the night's residual warmth. Then, bracing himself, he threw off the covers, swung his legs over the side of the bed and rested his bare feet on the rough planks. 'Today,' he decided, 'I must make a start.' Last night, tired out by his travels, he had stripped off his clothes and dropped them on the floor. This morning he selected the clothes which he considered most suitable for a day of exploration and unpacking. He splashed some water over his face and walked out into the hall.

Noises from the street burst in when he opened the front door. The roadway was full of people hurrying about their business, with a continuous babble of voices, the scraping of feet on worn cobblestones, the bleating of sheep wrapped around the shoulders of their shepherds, and the crowing of hens imprisoned in wicker baskets. All around there was an intoxicating smell of roasting meat and the scent of spices heaped on tables by the side of the road.

There was a watchtower at the top of the hill. The tower, he decided, would be the best place to see the layout of the town. He turned right out of the front door and headed up the hill. The cobbled street led to a flight of stone steps twisting upwards between wooden houses. Ahead, he watched as a young servant girl, her shapely arms full of fresh loaves, turned off the path into one of the houses. The door banged shut behind her. She had been there for a moment then was gone. He felt a pang of loneliness. He knew no one in Galata. In Venice, he couldn't walk along a street without someone calling out, 'Ciao, Nicolò, come stai oggi?'

He pressed on up the hill and reached the tower. Inside, the rooms were chilly. He climbed up the stone stairs. There were large rooms on each level given over to guardrooms and stores. On some floors there were Genoese guards grunting and coughing, looking as if they had fallen drunkenly asleep the night before, which indeed was probably what had happened. Nicolò passed between them and noted their lack of discipline and their ill manners. He was out of breath when he reached the gallery which ran around the top of the tower. He ducked his head to pass through a door into the fresh air.

He made a circuit of the gallery. Leaning over the railings, he could see, far below, merchant ships unloading their cargoes, and fishermen spreading out the night's catch. Housewives hurried up to buy what they needed for the day. From his vantage point, it was clear that the town of Galata was little more than a fortified camp. The outer defensive walls were thick, lined with cannon, and there were turrets at regular intervals. The houses of merchant families, his future patients he hoped, huddled within the protection of the walls. The flag of Genoa flew above the harbourmaster's office down below on the dock.

The city of Constantinople lay on the far side of the Golden Horn. A long line of interconnected towers, walls and castles ran along the seashore. An artist painting the scene would have used yellow ochre for the defensive walls, aqueducts and castles, and a sunlit iridescent white for the marble facades of the palaces, columns, and the cupolas of the churches, dotted around the hillside. The cobalt blue of the sea, broken up by lines of wind-ruffled waves, filled in the background. Beyond the city, the Princes' Islands, which they had passed yesterday in the galley, drew his eye across the Sea of Marmara to the village of Moda on the Asian shore.

He made his way down the tower. On an impulse, he decided to call in at a barber's shop. He was the only customer and the barber was pleased to welcome a client so unexpectedly and sat him down with effusive gestures. The man spoke only Greek, but a few gestures made it clear that Nicolò wanted him to cut his hair and trim his beard. Half an hour later he left the barber's feeling clean and civilised for the first time in weeks. It was time for breakfast! Bartoletti was waiting for him when he returned to the house: 'Master, breakfast is ready.'

They discussed plans over the meal, agreeing that the building in which they were lodged would be very suitable for the medical practice. It was a large wooden house located about halfway between the docks and the top of the hill and close to most of the residences from which they hoped to attract patients. The house had two large reception rooms on the ground floor which could be converted into a waiting room and a surgery. Behind the reception area were smaller rooms for a dispensary and an operating theatre. On the first floor were two recovery rooms for male and female patients post operation. There were also smaller rooms for administration and storage. Their personal accommodation would be on the second floor.

'We will need staff,' said Nicolò. 'Perhaps Signor Lomellino, the Podestà, could advise us. We are meeting him later.'

The Podestà was appointed by the city of Genoa to look after Genoese interests in Constantinople. His most important duty was to safeguard and expand the trading business of Genoa and to enforce its treaty rights. It was not his duty to help the Venetians to expand their businesses. The Podestà cultivated good relations with the Turks, particularly with Halil Pasha, the Sultan's Grand Vizier. The men had done profitable business together and were both wealthy as a result.

Nicolò was impressed at first by the Podestà's fine clothes and commanding presence. He wore a finely embroidered cloak and a chain of office around his neck, and was the sort of self-important man who expects to be treated with deference. But there was something about the man which Nicolò found unpleasant. His manners were a little too elaborate and his charm a little too practised. Later, Nicolò learned that the Podestà had "gone native" over the years, acquiring a love for oriental luxury and Byzantine intrigue. He kept a Greek mistress.

The Podestà raised no objections to their proposals for the practice. He agreed to help them recruit a practice nurse, receptionist and other helpers and volunteers. He recommended

Mary Celovic, their landlady, as a possible practice manager, and suggested that they visit the religious houses in Galata to see if they had brothers and sisters with nursing experience and find out if they could supply herbs for medicinal use. By the time the Podestà left, Nicolò was confident that setting up the practice would be fairly straightforward.

But Nicolò's most pressing task was to present the Doge's letters of introduction. The letters were addressed to the Emperor Constantine, the Grand Duke Loukas Notares, George Sphrantzes, historian and diplomat, Girolamo Minotto, Venetian representative in Constantinople, and Halil Pasha, Grand Vizier to Sultan Mehmed.

After breakfast, Nicolò sent Bartoletti to the Emperor's Blachernae Palace to arrange a meeting with Emperor Constantine, and the following week they took a ferry from Galata to Constantine's palace. The Golden Horn was packed with vessels of every size, shape and colour. They were rowed up the inlet past the church of Santa Sophia, the Jewish Quarter and the Spice Bazaar, and disembarked at the Xyloporta Gate through which they entered the city of Constantinople. The road from the ferry to the palace was dusty and in a poor state of repair and many of the houses were shuttered and empty.

Once inside the Blachaenae Palace, they were escorted by a secretary through a series of faded rooms. As their guide explained, the city had never fully recovered from being occupied by the Frankish soldiers of the Fourth Crusade some one hundred and fifty years earlier. The Crusaders had murdered and plundered their way through Constantinople and shipped its treasures to Western Europe. The plague of 1435 had added to the misery and decimated the population.

Constantine rose to greet his visitors. Nicolò bowed and presented the Doge's letter of introduction. The Emperor passed the letter to his secretary. He was a tall man aged about forty. His black beard was flecked with grey. His eyes were dark and had a fixed intensity and his eyebrows were thick and accentuated the dark circles under his eyes. He wore a full-length cloak lined with ermine. On his feet, he had the distinctive slippers worn only by the Byzantine Emperor.

All present treated Constantine with respect. After his father died, the court had agreed to his accession. His two brothers had been contenders for the throne, but they were not trusted to put aside their petty squabbles. Constantine was a serious man, dedicated to his duties as Roman Emperor, and a natural leader of men. He did not stand on ceremony, welcoming his visitors in a most friendly and informal manner.

'Ah, dottore, I have heard good reports of your work. We are most fortunate to have you with us. I fear we will soon have need of your services.'

Nicolò replied, 'Sire, I will serve you in any way I can.'

Constantine gestured towards the men standing with him. 'Let me introduce my most valued advisers – Loukas Notares, George Sphrantzes and Girolamo Minotto. I think you have letters of introduction for them as well.'

Nicolò gave each of them their copy of the Doge's letter, and Constantine explained the role of each adviser. 'The Grand Duke has been my trusted adviser for many years, particularly in matters of diplomacy and international agreements.'

Loukas Notares cast a cold eye on Nicolò, making the curtest of bows. His manner was dismissive towards the young doctor.

Constantine then turned to George Sphrantzes. 'This is my friend, George Sphrantzes. He has acted as my ambassador on many occasions. I am most grateful to him at the moment. He has returned from Georgia after finding me a new wife.'

George Sphrantzes had a bookish look about him. He seemed a man of ideas rather than a man of action. He wore dull clothes designed to keep him warm but without any attempt at fashion. Apparently his father had been a tutor to the former Emperor's children, and George himself had something of the schoolmaster about him. Constantine and George had been companions in their youth and they remained close friends.

'I was able to get a marriage contract signed off,' George explained. 'The daughter of the king of Georgia has agreed to become the wife of the Emperor and thus become Queen. She brings a dowry of thirty-six thousand gold coins plus an annual income of three thousand gold coins. This will be most useful at the present time. God willing, I will sail to Georgia to escort the young lady to Constantinople. My daughter, Tamar, will be a friend to her when she arrives.'

Constantine put an arm around George's shoulder. 'George, I am very grateful for your help.' And he turned to Minotto. 'Let me introduce Girolamo Minotto, who is Venetian bailor here in Constantinople. He is important to us in pressing our case for help before the Venetian Council. Perhaps you already know one another?'

Nicolò replied that he had not met Minotto but was pleased to do so. Minotto was dressed in court clothes. He greeted Nicolò in a most friendly manner. Constantine then surprised Nicolò. 'Dottore, we have given much thought to your role here in Constantinople. As you will know, the Turkish Sultan is

45

rumoured to be plotting to lay siege to our city. The man is young and inexperienced so may not be able to organise and carry out such an ambitious plan. However, we must prepare for the worst. I have established a Council of War consisting of my most trusted advisers, who will help me to prepare for the defence of the city. I should like you to attend the meetings as an adviser on medical matters when such advice is needed. You will be appointed medical officer to the navy to formalise your position. Would you be happy to act in that capacity?'

Nicolò replied that he would be pleased to assist in any way he could. He found himself once again drawn more deeply into the affairs of the Byzantine Empire than he had expected or would have wished. When would he pluck up courage to say no to such requests? He was becoming involved in a conflict which could end badly. Despite his reluctance, he felt attracted to the Byzantine cause. There was a romance about once glorious, now fading, empires and their emperors, which he found irresistible. At this point the audience ended, and Nicolò backed out of the Emperor's presence as convention required.

He and Bartoletti then made their way out of the palace. They were about to leave when George Sphrantzes caught up with them. 'Gentlemen, I should like to invite you to lunch today with myself and my family. My wife and children would like to meet you. It will just be a light meal al fresco.'

Nicolò accepted gratefully. They knew so few people in Constantinople and this invitation was a welcome and friendly gesture. George went ahead to warn his wife to expect visitors. The Sphrantzes family lived near the Church of the Holy Apostles, close to the Roman aqueduct which ran through the centre of the city, past the ruins of the forums of Theodosius and Constantine and the Hippodrome. Just beyond the Hippodrome they took a right turn off the Middle Road towards a group of substantial villas. A household servant guided them to the house.

George Sphrantzes was waiting at the entrance. They entered a generous hallway from which a central wooden staircase led to the first floor. As they entered, Helene, George's wife, came down the stairs with their two children – John and Tamar. Helene was, he guessed, in her late thirties. She was blessed with the classical beauty of a Greek woman. The bone structure of her face was finely drawn, and her skin was pale as marble. Her black hair was parted and braided on the crown of her head. The slender fingers she extended to him were thin and elegant as befitted a woman related to the Emperor. She had golden bangles about her wrists. Her eyes, framed by full eyebrows, were richly brown and fiercely intelligent. It mystified him how a dull and plain man like George could have secured such a beautiful wife.

The children were a delight. John was a youth of eleven full of infectious energy and enthusiasm. Tamar was not so obviously beautiful, but her face was full of warmth and liveliness, and her thoughts and emotions ran flickering across it like sunlight under an apple tree. Nicolò could imagine her following in her father's footsteps and becoming a scholar. She was ten years old. The children shared all their pleasures and enthusiasms with one another. Today they were excited at having visitors from Venice, which was a place they longed to visit. They asked many questions about Nicolò's work as a doctor and about life in Venice. John wanted details of the operations which Nicolò had performed on board ship. They confided in Nicolò and Bartoletti, with charming openness, their personal hopes and expectations.

They lunched in the garden. It was warm enough even in November to sit outside at a long wooden table within a vine-covered arbour. The household servants put on the table platters of mezze, fish, fruit and bread, with bowls of olive oil for dipping chunks of newly baked bread. There were carafes of chilled white wine and jugs of water drawn from the cold water of the aqueduct.

During the lunch, George recounted tales of his recent travels in Georgia. He amused them by telling scandalous stories of court life and the difficulties of finding Constantine a suitable wife. George explained that he always told prospective brides the truth and made it clear to them that the Emperor was much older than they were and that he had been married twice before. He showed the young women a portrait of Constantine and assured them that he was a brave knight and a kindly man. After two years of negotiations, Matilde, daughter of the king of Georgia, had agreed to marry Constantine, with the active encouragement of her parents.

The king of Georgia had asked that Tamar should be a friend to Matilde when she reached Constantinople. George willingly agreed. In return, the king of Georgia promised to provide Tamar with a dowry when she got married. Tamar was delighted to hear this. She would be happy to welcome Matilde, of course, but the promise of her own dowry would secure her future happiness. She flung her arms around George's neck and thanked her father.

John had not been forgotten either. The king of Georgia had sent him a finely wrought sword as a present. George intended to take John with him when he returned to Georgia to fetch Constantine's bride. John hoped that this mission could be the start of a diplomatic career following in his father's footsteps.

It was on this optimistic note that lunch ended. The children left the table chattering excitedly, walking arm in arm across the garden and into the house. They planned to meet with two of the Notares children later in the afternoon. But when they went, they carried away some of the happiness of the day. The adults fell silent as they watched them go.

George said, 'We cannot be sure what the situation will be by next spring. If the Turks lay siege to the city, the wedding may have to be postponed or even cancelled. The king of Georgia would not want his daughter to marry Constantine in such circumstances. What do you think, dottore?'

Responding, Nicolò said, 'My opinion does not count for much. I have been here only a short time. Most people I have spoken to think there will be no siege.'

Helene then interrupted him. 'I, too, have talked to my friends. Many are planning to leave Constantinople. They want their children to be safe even if their husbands have to stay and fight. I must tell you, dottore, that my husband will not allow us to leave. He thinks that the Emperor would see it as a betrayal, but Constantine has no children. His loyalty is to the Byzantine Empire. I fear that my husband's loyalty is to the Emperor rather than to myself and the children.'

Nicolò hesitated. 'I am not married, madame, and have neither wife nor children. But if the opportunity to escape presented itself, when defeat seemed certain, then I think I should want my wife and children out of harm's way.'

George was finding this conversation embarrassing. 'Helene, you may be sure I will do everything I can to protect you and the children. I remain optimistic that we will see off the Turks. If the worst comes to the worst, I will arrange for a ship to take you to Chios to stay with your family, but I will have to stay by the Emperor's side as long as he needs me.'

Nicolò and Bartoletti left shortly afterwards. It had been a pleasure to be with a family once more. Hopefully they would be invited again. But would the circumstances permit? The future looked increasingly uncertain. Everyone was worried. The two men walked down to the ferry, which was a fishing boat rowed by four men and steered by an oar at the stern. The currents were too strong to allow the ferry to cross directly so they had to head across and up the Golden Horn, then pick up the reverse current which carried the boat across to the dock at Galata. The ferry ride took twenty minutes. The evening sun lit up the buildings of the old city behind them. They were pleased to get back to the house in Galata which was already beginning to feel like home. Mary's servant had prepared supper for them. After supper, Nicolò wrote his report.

Report to the Doge:
15 November 1451

Your Excellency,
I can report that I have presented the letters of introduction to Emperor Constantine, Loukas Notares and George Sphrantzes. I will deliver your letter to Halil Pasha as soon as it can be arranged.

The Emperor has appointed me as medical officer to the navy. He has asked me to attend Council meetings to advise on medical facilities should there be war with the Turks. No one really knows how the situation will develop but all are nervous as to the Sultan's intentions. Things will become clearer in the next few weeks. I will keep you updated as soon as there is further news.

Your respectful servant,
Dot. Nicolò Barbaro

4

Throat Cutter on the Bosphorus
1451–1452

 he Podestà asked Nicolò, 'Have you read the Doge's letter of introduction addressed to Halil Pasha? It might contain a coded message so we should take great care. Let me read it.'

Nicolò reluctantly handed the letter over. He was not sure he could trust the Podestà, but he needed his help to arrange a meeting with Halil Pasha.

The Podestà read the letter and bestowed a patronising smile on Nicolò. 'Well, it explains that you did research at Padua University and that you hope to exchange your research findings with Turkish scholars for the mutual advancement of medicine.

I cannot see any hidden messages, invisible ink or ciphers. The writer has been careful, but my advice would be to avoid any direct contact with the Turks except through myself.'

'Thank you for your advice, Podestà,' Nicolò replied firmly, 'but the Doge ordered me to deliver it in person. Besides, I should like to meet Halil Pasha. What can you tell me about him?'

'I will tell you what I know,' the Podestà replied. 'Halil Pasha was Grand Vizier to the late Sultan Murad. It was he who advised Sultan Murad in 1422, thirty years ago, to call off the previous siege of Constantinople. Sultan Murad waged war in self-defence and attacked no one except with good reason, preferring negotiation to fighting wars. As he aged, Sultan Murad was increasingly drawn to a life of contemplation. He gave up the throne in favour of his son, Mehmed, and retreated to the country.

Mehmed was only thirteen at the time and, perhaps through inexperience after becoming Sultan, managed to offend both the religious clerics and the Janissaries. A sultan is an absolute ruler but he needs the support of the clergy and the Janissaries to stay in power. The political situation became so unstable that Murad deposed his son on the recommendation of Halil Pasha and resumed the throne.'

'Then why did Mehmed confirm Halil Pasha as Grand Vizier when he became Sultan?' Nicolò asked.

'I was at the ceremony in Adrianople when Mehmed became Sultan after his father died,' the Podestà replied. 'Halil Pasha, out of fear of the young Sultan's anger, tried to lose himself in the throng of courtiers, but Ottoman etiquette dictates that at such ceremonies each official must wear distinctive clothing and stand in their traditional spot. Mehmed noticed immediately that Halil

Pasha was not in his usual place and asked the Chief Eunuch to summon him. Mehmed graciously allowed Halil Pasha to kiss his hand and confirmed his appointment as his Grand Vizier. After the ceremony, Halil Pasha confided to me his fear that the Sultan would one day take revenge on him for his role in Mehmed's humiliating deposition. 'Mehmed neither forgets nor forgives,' were his words. The man lives in constant fear that one morning the Sultan's executioners will knock on his door with orders to strangle him.'

The Podestà arranged to meet Halil Pasha in Bursa to discuss trade matters and suggested that Nicolò might join them. Two weeks later, at the end of November, Nicolò, Bartoletti and the Podestà sailed from Galata to the town of Yalova on the Asian shore. The voyage took all night and was followed by a three-hour ride from Yalova to Bursa, the former Ottoman capital. The morning air was chilly, but the sky was clear, making an invigorating start to the day. The town of Bursa was set in pleasant rolling country which rose into the nearby hills and mountains. From the market place, they could see snow glistening on the summit of Mount Olympus. Wagons carrying blocks of ice cut from the mountain's couloirs trundled through the marketplace on their way to Constantinople.

Halil Pasha welcomed them at the city gate. The Vizier was an impressive figure in his white turban, flowing black gown and insignia of office. He had a carefully barbered beard and his eyes were concentrated, missing nothing. The impression he gave was of a fastidious and confident man used to commanding others. He read the letter of introduction but made no comment.

'Welcome to Bursa, my friends,' he said smoothly. The welcoming smile was intended to reassure and to hint at the possibility of reaching an understanding. 'Now I should like you to come with me to the Janissary camp to enjoy a formal parade in your honour. Then we can eat a relaxing lunch to discuss matters of common interest, after which, in the evening, you can return to Constantinople. Is that programme acceptable to you?'

All agreed that this was entirely satisfactory, hoping that such a civilised reception would result in improved relations between the two sides. As guests of Halil Pasha, they were given an enthusiastic welcome by a guard of honour of one hundred horsemen. The mounted cavalry carried brightly coloured shields, lances and jewelled scimitars. Their turbans were multi-coloured or pure white depending on rank. The horses were splendid animals with shining high-backed saddles, polished leather reins, glinting stirrups and jangling bridles. The Turkish cavalry paraded at the walk, then at the trot. The horsemen demonstrated their skill in sticking targets with their lances and, finally, at full gallop charged with gleaming scimitars, slicing down onto the heads of imaginary enemies. It was difficult not to be impressed.

The Janissary camp was laid out in ordered rows. Each section was assigned to a separate platoon, regiment and division in much the same way as the Romans had set out their camps. It was orderly, disciplined and had a quiet calm. There were no drunken soldiers nor evidence of ill-discipline. They witnessed no quarrelling, merrymaking, drinking or gambling as was customary in Byzantine camps. Even the latrines were freshly dug each day. Overall they thought that the Turkish troops projected the quiet confidence that comes from habituation to victory, endurance, frugality and watchfulness. This, of course, was the impression which Halil Pasha wanted to convey.

The contrast to the Byzantine army was stark. As Bartoletti observed, based on his own military service, the Byzantine army lacked discipline, proper training and endurance. It had a reputation for insubordination, licence, drunkenness and debauchery. The officers were motivated more by avarice than by duty. Many of the troops were foreign mercenaries; such men were paid to fight but did not expect to lay down their lives for their paymasters.

At midday, a meal was set out in a tent for the visitors and their hosts. There were bowls of yoghurt and fruit, including peaches, figs, raisins and cherries. Large platters of rice with mutton were shared by visitors and hosts. The meat course was followed by a dessert of honey and sorbet cooled in the ice brought down from Mount Olympus.

There was plenty of opportunity for the two sides to exchange frank views on current affairs without giving offence. There were smiles all round and cheerful conversation. After lunch, under an increasingly cloudy sky, Halil Pasha accompanied them some of the way to the port where they were to embark for Constantinople.

'Halil Pasha,' said Nicolò, 'thank you for your most generous hospitality. We were very impressed by the military displays. We have not had much time to discuss medical matters but rest assured that we would welcome exchanges of information with your doctors.'

'I will arrange for our doctors to meet with you shortly,' replied Halil Pasha, warmly embracing the young doctor.

On the voyage back to Galata, the wind swung round to the north and its cold blast hinted at the coming winter. The companions exchanged notes on what they had seen. They were concerned at the high quality and number of Turkish troops.

The Ottomans seemed to have the means to mount an attack on Constantinople with no shortage of men, money and other resources. The contrast with the Byzantine position was painful.

As Bartoletti put it, 'The Turks pour from the Asian steppe like a river in flood. They can make good any losses in battle. They grow stronger by the day.'

It was on this rather dismal note that they parted on reaching Galata. The Podestà was not surprised by their comments for he had seen for himself the quality of Turkish fighting men. He had concluded long ago that it was in his personal interest to keep on friendly terms with Halil Pasha. In fact, he proclaimed his loyalty to the Emperor while keeping the Turks informed about Byzantine plans.

Nicolò took advantage of Halil Pasha's invitation to meet some of the Ottoman doctors. It was a chance to see how advanced their medicine was compared to that of the West. There were areas where he could improve his practice to take advantage of their advances particularly in the field of herbal remedies. Over these early months in Galata his knowledge expanded considerably. Neither he nor the Ottoman doctors he talked to felt they were in competition but rather that improving medical practice would be used for the benefit of all humanity. Nicolò introduced these advances into his Galata practice for the benefit of the families living there. The application of new medical practice to the military and naval forces seemed to him to be of secondary importance.

In March 1452, six months after the visit to Bursa the Podestà asked Nicolò if he and Bartoletti would be willing to undertake a reconnaissance of the area where a castle was to be built which was about five miles from the city and close to the village of Bebek.

'You can disguise yourselves as fishermen. If it is safe to do so, you could land and talk to the villagers to find out what is happening. Keep careful notes and make diagrams of any construction.'

Here was an opportunity for real adventure. Nicolò persuaded a reluctant Bartoletti to go with him much against the latter's better judgement since he disliked the idea of taking a small fishing boat up the Bosphorus at night. However, two weeks later, at midnight, Nicolò and Bartoletti boarded a fishing boat moored in Galata. It was a sturdy wooden craft about twenty feet in length, with a covered section in the bow. There were two benches for rowing and a mast and sail. The interior of the boat was crammed with sails, nets, ropes and fish baskets. There were three crew – the fisherman and his two sons. Fishing was their livelihood and they knew these waters down to the last treacherous eddy.

'We will take them,' the fisherman agreed, 'but if we run into problems with the Turks, we will pitch the Venetian dogs over the side.'

The Podestà raised no objections to their doing this. He had no interest in helping the Venetians.

The small boat cast off. Weather conditions were poor, with a strong, blustery wind blowing down the Bosphorus from the Black Sea. The boat rolled alarmingly and short, steep waves smacked over the gunwales into the bottom of the boat. The fishermen altered course to head more directly into the wind. The rolling became a pitching motion. Bartoletti retreated to the shelter under the bows and curled up miserably, much to the amusement of the Greek fishermen. When they reached Leander's Tower near the Asian shore, the water became calmer and they were able to raise the lateen sail. As dawn broke, they joined the other fishing boats off the old castle of Anadolu Hisar on the Asian shore opposite Bebek. One of the fishermen spotted a shoal of mackerel churning the water about half a mile away. Seabirds wheeled and dived frantically. The other fishing boats hauled in the unexpected bounty and turned back for Galata when they had filled their nets. They raced one another to be the first fishermen to start selling their catch in the morning market.

The black of night had given way to a grey dawn and the hills on the European shore emerged from the night. They could see sheep and goats grazing between wooden huts. Farmers came out of the houses, stretching in the damp cold of the morning air. The cottagers stared out across the water at the fishing boats.

On the European shore, jagged and incomplete, the skeleton of a fortress rose menacingly from the fast-running water. As they watched, a line of barges filled with rock, stone, wood and assorted construction materials passed to their starboard. The barges made for a jetty on the European side where a number of transports were tied up. It was early morning but already labourers were moving the cargo from the transports to the construction site. On the shore there was a partially completed tower from which outer walls climbed up to join with a similar tower at the top of the hill. In total they counted fifteen towers under construction. The fort was only partly completed, but it did not take much imagination to realise that, when finished, this new fortress would present a formidable challenge. Its purpose could only be to cut off supplies to the city of Constantinople. The despairing people of Constantinople later nicknamed it the "Throat Cutter" because its construction was the first step in starving them into submission.

They turned away from the rest of the fishing fleet into Bebek harbour. The crew, always alert to commercial opportunities, started selling their mackerel to the villagers. Meanwhile, Nicolò and Bartoletti got into conversation with an elderly Greek fisherman. He told them that the Turkish survey teams had arrived unexpectedly in February 1452. The surveyors did not explain why a survey was needed except that it was work commissioned by Sultan Mehmed.

'We knew it was to be something big,' the Greek told them, 'when thousands of workers started arriving from all over the country, and construction materials piled up. The Turks built a camp to house the workers and posted guards over the site night and day. The soldiers destroyed our homes and villages. These hyenas stole our food and our animals. We and our families faced starvation. Some of our young men, hotheads, ganged together to attack the Turkish patrols and, in the fighting, a number of Turks were killed. The Ottomans exacted revenge. Early one morning the farmers were ploughing the fields when Turkish cavalry charged out from nearby woods. The peasants fled in panic but were caught and trampled under hoof or cut down by scimitars as the cavalry charged over the top of them. Women and children hiding in the village were not spared. Only a handful of us fishermen survived because we were out in our boats.'

Nicolò decided they had seen enough. It was time to follow the other fishing boats and return to Galata before the Ottomans became suspicious. The wind was favourable and they made good time. By midday they had reached Galata and told the Podestà what they had seen.

'It is as I feared,' the Podestà commented. 'First cut off your enemy's supply lines then advance on his city.'

Nicolò said, 'No one came to defend the villagers from the Turks. Surely it is the duty of a Christian emperor to protect his subjects. If he can no longer protect them, what legitimacy does the Emperor have left?'

'There are those,' replied the Podestà, 'who think that since the Byzantine Empire is too weak to defend its own people, we would be better off under a Turkish Sultan. Does that shock you, young man?'

'Yes, I do find it shocking that people would prefer being ruled by the Sultan rather than the Emperor. Do they put so low a value on their Christian faith? How could anyone want to be ruled by a tyrant?'

'There are many possible reasons,' replied the Podestà, 'but freedom from Byzantine taxes and corruption are strong motivations. They might well be better off under the Sultan.'

The castle was completed by September 1452. It was a formidable fortification. The Sultan issued instructions that all vessels passing the castle must lower their sails to await the arrival of customs officers and pay the transit fees. Any ships failing to stop would be caught in the crossfire from the two castles.

The owners of the trading galleys resented the new imposts. Some skippers were willing to risk it, relying on their seamanship to get past the forts. In early November two galleys reached Constantinople to much celebration. Some weeks later another three galleys tried to repeat the feat. They came down the Bosphorus from the Black Sea, driven by the strong current and favourable winds. The first two ships passed unscathed and sailed on to Constantinople. The third ship, the *San Marco*, followed, but the garrison commander had by then reloaded his cannon. The first shot skimmed low over the sea hitting the galley amidships and it started to sink. Most of the crew were drowned or swept away by the currents. A Turkish customs board rescued fourteen men including Nicolò's friend Captain Risso. The prisoners were taken under military escort to Adrianople to await the Sultan's decision as to their punishment. Mehmed wanted to make an example of these men who had defied his orders. Twelve of the crew were beheaded and their heads set on spikes along the city walls of Adrianople. Captain Risso was impaled on a wooden stake driven through his stomach and under his ribcage. The stake holding Risso's live body was set up outside the city gate as a warning to others who defied the Sultan. His terrible death some hours later was witnessed by passers-by. His corpse was left to rot.

The youngest member of the crew, a boy, was released near Constantinople to ensure that the news of the executions was reported to the Byzantines. The terror tactics worked. Ships paid their dues from then on. All agreed that the young sultan was a man to be feared.

Report to the Doge:
30 November 1452

Your Excellency,
I can confirm that I have delivered your letter of introduction to the Grand Vizier Halil Pasha who invited us to meet him at Bursa. He laid on a most impressive display by a troop of Turkish cavalry. He showed us around a Janissary encampment where the Turkish troops were disciplined and well equipped. The camp itself was clean and ordered. He told us that there was no shortage of fresh troops available if and when needed.

There has been a major addition to the fortifications along the Bosphorus. The Turks have built a new castle opposite the old castle at Anadolu Hisar. The effect is that the Ottomans now control all supplies coming from the Black Sea to Constantinople. The citizens of Constantinople have named the castle "The Throat Cutter" because it will cut off food and other supplies to the city.

The crew who survived the sinking of the San Marco were murdered in cold blood, including Captain Risso, the much admired captain of the San Marco. The citizens fear death and destruction if a siege is successful. Reinforcements are urgently needed. Please do all you can to provide them. The situation grows darker and more threatening by the day.

Your respectful servant,
Dot. Nicolò Barbaro

5

Mehmed Plans The Siege
1452

he Grand Vizier, Halil Pasha, left Bursa after his meeting with the Podestà and the Venetian doctor. The meeting confirmed his view that the Byzantines were ill prepared for war. He knew, from other informants, that Byzantine resources of men and money were in short supply and that they could not afford to buy new cannon. However, he was a cautious man and knew it would be foolish to assume that Constantinople was ripe for the plucking, or that taking the city would be a simple task. The great walls of Constantinople had frustrated enemies for many centuries.

Halil Pasha returned to Adrianople with foreboding for he was afraid of Mehmed. However, he did not have an audience that night so he went to bed worn out by his travels, with his wife by his side. She was a good woman, wise and discreet, the daughter of a Hungarian nobleman who had been killed in war with the Turks. Having been taken prisoner, she was sold to the Sultan Murad who then gifted her to Halil Pasha. She was the one person for whom he had a deep affection and he trusted her completely.

In the middle of the night he was woken by a loud and peremptory banging on the door. He tried to ignore the noise, but a brutal voice yelled out, 'Get up. The Sultan wants to see you right now.'

The door to the bedroom crashed open. In the doorway stood the Black Aga, Chief Eunuch at the court of Sultan Mehmed, procurer of young girls and boys for the Sultan's pleasure and one of his most feared executioners.

Halil's wife sat bolt upright in terror. 'Is the Sultan angry with you, husband? May Allah have mercy on us.'

She was shaking uncontrollably, quite certain that the Black Aga had come to kill her husband. It is in the dead of night that tyrants settle scores, and men like the Black Aga obeyed orders without question and, indeed, took pleasure in their work.

'Get up,' yelled the Black Aga. The man's smooth and bloated Nubian body filled the doorway. The Sultan's executioner was sweating profusely and his repellent reek filled the room.

Halil's wife wrapped a cloak around her husband's thin and ageing body. She tried to cling to him, but the loathsome eunuch pushed her away.

'Follow me,' he ordered.

Halil's wife just had time to thrust a box containing gold coins into her husband's hands.

'Take this, husband – bargain for your life.'

Clutching the box, Halil Pasha followed the Black Aga into the palace garden. There he breathed deeply of the jasmine-scented night air as if he was taking his last breath. Nightingales called to one another from the cypress trees which lined the path. Wicker lamps hanging from the trees threw shadowy lights across the garden, heightening the sense of unreality as he hurried to his doom. He could hear running water which made a pleasing sound like the rippling of water over stones in a country stream. Just for an instant, Halil Pasha felt calm and more composed, but it was not to last for at the end of the path they entered the Sultan's private apartments. The rooms inside were dark, musty and claustrophobic. At the end of a passageway he saw a light under a door. The Black Aga knocked, opened the door and pushed Halil Pasha into the room.

Sultan Mehmed was sitting cross-legged on a pile of cushions, surrounded by maps, books, drawings and handwritten notes. Mehmed neither moved nor acknowledged his visitor's arrival. He has been there all night, thought Halil Pasha. He had known Mehmed as a boy but had never felt any affection for him. The youth had been wilful and disobedient, too remote and too cold. He doubted if Mehmed felt affection for anyone other than himself. His eyes were black and no light or warmth escaped that blackness. He did not smile. The long hook of a nose accentuated the intensity of his eyes. He wore a white turban and scarf around his neck, a padded shirt to ward off the night chill, and a blue fur-lined cloak. It was his stillness that frightened Halil Pasha most. Halil Pasha put the chest of gold on a side table close to the Sultan.

'What is that?' demanded Mehmed.

Halil Pasha blustered, 'Custom decrees that when a noble is summoned to his master at an unusual hour, he must not appear with empty hands.'

The Sultan knew fear when he saw it. The man was offering him a bribe to save his worthless life. Mehmed inspired terror in all who came close to him, for one gesture from him was enough to condemn a man to an agonising death. He had got used to and enjoyed this power over life and death. Already the number of his victims stretched the length of many corridors. Sometimes he feared the revenge of these ghosts and their families, but he was so steeped in blood that there was no going back, nor did he wish to turn back.

'I don't need your gifts, but leave the box there. I want to discuss with you my plans to take Constantinople. You can help or hinder me. If you help me, I can promise you honours and gifts beyond measure. If you fail me...'

Mehmed's voice tailed off. Halil Pasha knew only too well what would happen to him if he failed.

'I will not fail you, sire.' He grovelled with a deep bow.

'You failed my father,' the Sultan said quietly in a voice full of menace. 'My people will be watching you closely to make sure you are loyal to me and not to your friends among the Crusader dogs.'

'Sire, I have no such friends. I have only diplomatic contacts, such as the Podestà of Galata, who supply me with valuable information.'

'Good,' replied Mehmed. 'I demand absolute loyalty. As you will have noticed,' Mehmed gestured towards the piles of maps and papers on the bed, 'I have studied the previous attempts to capture the city. The main reasons for our past failures are, in my opinion, firstly, that the city continued to receive supplies, despite blockades, and secondly, our siege guns were not powerful enough to bring down the walls. As for the first, I have already commissioned the building of the fort on the European shore which will enable us to cut off supplies to Constantinople. You and your fellow viziers, Saruca, Zaganos and Sihabeddin, have paid for the towers and your share of the six thousand skilled workers. I know that you have made yourselves rich at my expense, so you can afford it. The target date for completion is the end of September this year. I will accept no excuses for failure to meet this deadline.'

Halil Pasha assured the Sultan, 'We have the project in hand, sire. There have been a number of protests by local farmers, but these have been dealt with and the work continues on schedule.'

'Good,' said Mehmed. 'The second problem is that of siege artillery. I have been approached by a cannon builder whose name is Orbán of Hungary. My spies tell me that he has already offered to supply Emperor Constantine, but the Byzantines could not afford his price. He claims that his designs are for cannons with longer range, greater weight of shot and quicker reloading than any previously available. The man is waiting outside to see us.'

The Black Aga showed Orbán in. The arms merchant walked confidently into the room. He was not overawed by being in the presence of a sultan. He had something to sell which this Sultan needed. The Sultan had to have his cannon to bring down the walls of Constantinople and there were no other cannons which could do the job, or so he claimed. He knew that cost did not matter to ambitious men like Mehmed. Victory was all that mattered. Arms suppliers thrive in such situations.

Orbán was a tall man with the broad shoulders of a peasant. His hair was long and black, slightly greasy and thinned into strands which hung limply over his ears. His beard was turning grey. The face was full and heavy with a large hooked nose. His skin was coarse and his eyes were grey under overhanging lids, which gave him a sly look. He wore clothes woven from thick charcoal cloth. He looked like a man who knew his business and would strike a hard bargain.

'Let me see your technical drawings,' demanded Mehmed.

They moved over to a large table on which Orbán unrolled his designs under a lamp. The two men leaned over the drawings. They entered into detailed discussions of gun sizes, range, weight of shot, techniques for reloading and time between firings. Orbán was impressed by Mehmed's engineering knowledge and grasp of detail.

'Can you make me a cannon to fire a missile weighing twelve hundred pounds with a range of over a mile?' asked Mehmed.

'I can build such a cannon. It will be the longest and most powerful cannon ever built, but my designs allow for that. The gun would have to be twenty-six feet long and weigh twenty tons. It will be a monster, but that is what you are going to need,' replied Orbán. 'I can build you any gun you wish provided you can pay. It will cost a lot of money.'

Mehmed gave Halil Pasha his orders: 'Halil Pasha, draw up a contract for two of the longest cannon plus a number of smaller pieces. Agree the price. Delivery must not be later than four months from signing the contract. Make sure that Orbán has all the resources and facilities he needs to complete the job. The work must be done here in Adrianople. Payment will be contingent, of course, on satisfactory performance and testing. One important condition, Orbán, is that you must not work for the Emperor Constantine under any circumstance. You will assign all rights in the technical designs to me. You will deliver on time. No excuses will be accepted. Any breach of my conditions would be a serious matter. Do you understand?'

Mehmed was looking directly at Orbán. There could be no doubt in Orbán's mind that he would be foolish to cross this Sultan, and he put aside thoughts of trying his usual fraudulent tricks, deceptions and price increases. Contracts were exchanged within the week.

In four months the cannon was ready for its test firing. The gun was winched onto a huge wooden sledge and teams of oxen were used to pull it to the firing position. The barrel was elevated to fifteen degrees above the horizontal, aiming in the direction of an earth bank just beneath the walls of Adrianople. The gunners rammed coarse black gunpowder into the barrel, followed by wadding to hold the powder in place. The stone shot was pushed into the barrel and the fuse was lit. There was a tremendous roar which shocked the gunners and the townspeople. They thought the force had split the bronze barrel, but when the smoke cleared it was still intact. The observers followed the shot as it curved up and through the evening sky. It hit the earth bank with a thud, shaking the city wall. Clouds of acrid smoke poured from the barrel. The smoke rolled across the plain and climbed up over the walls, filling the streets and alleyways of the town and choking the people. No one cheered, so shocked were they by the noise and power of the weapon.

'Congratulations, Orbán,' exclaimed a delighted Mehmed. 'Now I am confident the city of Constantinople will soon be mine.'

A few days later, two ambassadors from the Emperor arrived in Adrianople. Halil Pasha welcomed them. Gifts were exchanged, and then they explained the reasons for requesting a meeting. They were there to demand a substantial increase in the fee that the Byzantines were paid by the Ottomans for holding Prince Orhan captive in Constantinople. Orhan was a possible rival claimant to the Sultan's throne, so keeping him in custody was important to the Sultan. The Emperor's advisory council saw Sultan Murad's recent death as an opportunity to increase the annual fee. Halil Pasha informed Mehmed of their visit. Surprisingly, the Sultan was calm.

'Let them demand, but pay them nothing. It is in our interest to let them believe we can be bullied into meeting their demands. At the moment, we will play their game and I have agreed to renew all the treaties signed by my father. They imagine I am a soft touch. Let them think that for now. When we are ready, they will realise their mistake.'

Once the cannon had been tested and the "Throat Cutter" fort completed in late 1452, the Turks changed their tune. When the ambassadors returned once more to press the case for an increase in fee, the Sultan ordered that they be beheaded and their heads sent back to the Emperor stuffed with straw. The message was clear. The Sultan did not negotiate. The execution of the ambassadors was a declaration of war.

Report to the Doge:
2 December 1452

Your Excellency,
I can confirm that the new Bosphorus fort has been completed by

the Ottomans. Supplies from the Black Sea reach Constantinople only with the permission of the Sultan. Ships refusing to obey the Turks pay a heavy price not only with money but with the lives of their crews.

I have received reports that the Turks are developing more powerful artillery built with the help of a Hungarian engineer. The new cannon could make all the difference between success and failure if the Turks lay siege to Constantinople. The Emperor has nothing to match these guns.

There is growing evidence that the Turks intend to besiege Constantinople. The Emperor needs help from his allies. Please do all you can to provide men, weapons, food and other supplies to the city for the citizens grow more desperate with each passing day.

Unfortunately, the Byzantines are their own worst enemies. They demanded an increase in the fee for holding Prince Orhan. They do not seem to understand that they are in no position to make demands. It seems to me a misjudged and arrogant demand made by the Emperor's council. I think Loukas Notares is behind it. He is convinced that his aggressive approach will pay off. I fear he will be proved wrong. The Sultan shows no sign of yielding to pressure and has just executed the Emperor's ambassadors.

Your respectful servant,
Dot. Nicolò Barbaro

6

Constantine Seeks Help

he Emperor called a meeting of his council to decide how best to respond to the execution of the two ambassadors and how to secure more help from his western allies.

<u>Minutes of a Meeting of Council.</u>

Held at: the Blachernai Palace, Constantinople.

Date: November 30 1452.

Chairman: The Emperor Constantine.

In Attendance: Loukas Notares – Grand Admiral, George

Sphrantzes – Secretary to the Council, Archbishop Isadore – Papal Legate, Nicolò Barbaro – Medical Officer to the Navy, and other senior administrators, naval and military commanders.

Emperor Constantine expressed his outrage at the execution of the two ambassadors:

'It was a barbaric act contrary to the rules of diplomatic immunity and the code of chivalry. We have been seduced by the Sultan's assurance that the treaties made by his father would be honoured. The Sultan swore to me on the Holy Koran that he would respect the integrity of Byzantine territory. It is clear to me now that he had no intention of doing any such thing. We have all failed to understand the Sultan's true character. Council advised me that we should increase the fee we charge the Turks for holding Prince Orhan. By killing the ambassadors, Sultan Mehmed has called our bluff, and since we cannot enforce our demands, our weakness is clear for all to see. I was poorly advised by Council.'

Loukas Notares wanted to avoid a discussion as to who was to blame for the fee debacle. He replied:

'The death of these two men is, of course, regrettable but this council has more important concerns. The construction of the new Ottoman castle on the European shore, in combination with the present castle on the Asian shore, will permit the Sultan to control the flow of men and weapons along the Bosphorus. To demonstrate his power, Sultan Mehmed has marched fifty thousand troops along the European shore to the city walls, and he camped there for three days studying our defences. Now he has gone to Adrianople to finalise his plans but left the Turkish fleet anchored off Moda in full view of the city to undermine the morale of our citizens. We have all heard the people's dismal chant: "This is the end of the city. These are the omens of the end of our race. These are the days of the Antichrist." The people are right to be afraid. There is a huge disparity between Byzantine and Ottoman forces in terms of firepower and numbers of troops.'

Nicolò Barbaro unwisely interrupted: 'Each day, from the top of the Galata Tower, I have watched the Turks moving along the European shore. As they advance they torch the villages. The coast road is jammed with refugees and buffalo carts piled with household possessions. Old people collapse by the roadside. The Turks advance towards Constantinople like the pestilence – terrifying, silent and quite deadly.'

Notares administered the young doctor a sharp put-down. 'Young man, we have heard enough of your negativity. We will defeat the Turks as we have done in the past. Your job is to advise us on medical matters. Tell us what preparations you have made in that regard.'

Nicolò was embarrassed. He was being challenged to explain himself in front of the Emperor. The room fell silent. Everyone knew Notares was trying to humiliate the young man. The councillors looked down at their papers in embarrassment.

'Gentlemen, there is still much to do, I admit it. In outline, my plan is that routine medical needs will be met by our practice in Galata and that a field hospital will be set up for treating war wounded in Constantinople. I am working through the details and will bring my plan to Council within the month.'

Loukas Notares smiled to himself. He had made his point. The upstart young Venetian was failing to deliver. Constantine knew Loukas Notares to be a capable but an unpleasant and dismissive man. He wanted to save Nicolò's face, and said, 'I look forward to seeing your proposal when it is completed.'

The Emperor then moved the discussions onto reinforcements to be expected from western allies.

'Venice is our best hope. There are Venetian trading galleys moored in the Golden Horn, but we have to persuade them to remain. The captains want to sail to get clear of Constantinople before the Turks impose a blockade. To encourage them to remain, I propose we pay each ship four hundred ducats a month and feed the crews. So far, three merchant galleys and two light galleys have agreed to stay on these terms.'

Archbishop Isadore commented, 'If these five galleys remain there is no danger this winter that Turkish ships will come to assault our harbour or make attacks in any other way.'

Constantine continued, 'I have also offered to compensate ship owners for loss of profits. Venice will be informed of these arrangements. Other merchant vessels will be allowed to leave. The support of the Pope is our next best hope, but the Pope's help is conditional on the reunification of the Roman and Orthodox churches. The people are strongly opposed to closer ties to Rome, but reunification is imperative if we want Papal assistance. I ask Council to approve the holding of a reunification service as soon as possible.'

Council agreed to the holding of the service of reunification on the thirteenth of December in Santa Sophia, and to making the proposed payments to the Venetian ships. The meeting ended just as the evening light was fading. Chairs were pushed back with a great deal of noisy scraping of wood on the stone floor. Groups of councillors exited the hall talking quietly among themselves. The meeting had done nothing to raise morale.

Nicolò and Bartoletti took the ferry back to Galata. The following day, Nicolò called a meeting at the Galata practice.

He addressed the staff: 'We must assume that the Turks will soon lay siege to the city. If that happens you must be prepared to continue to work here without me. I will be committed to treating the wounded at the field hospital in Constantinople, and Bartoletti and I will spend most of our time in Constantinople. We will return to Galata only when there is a lull in the fighting. I am pleased to tell you that Mary Celovic has agreed to administer the practice in my absence. She will look after the staff, make patients' appointments, ensure that medicines are in stock and keep the detailed records of operations and treatments. The sisters from the Franciscan convent will work with her. However, I must point out that there are risks for you all if you continue working here. If the Turks take the city they will punish those who have worked in this practice for the Emperor. Each of you must weigh the risks. I will understand it if any of you wish to leave the practice.'

All the staff confirmed that they would continue to work there whatever the personal risk. The staff meeting ended at this point, but no one was left in any doubt as to the gravity of the situation.

Some of the women resented the promotion of Mary Celovic. There were whispers that the dottore favoured Mary Celovic too much, and there was even speculation that there might be a romantic attachment.

Mary dismissed all such speculation with a smile. 'Of course not! Where did you get such an idea? I like him and admire his medical work, that's all. Well, everyone likes the dottore, don't they?'

The answer to that question was that the young women found him attractive and unreasonably good-looking and that the older married ladies wanted to mother him. The men thought that he did a good job and looked out for their interests. As for Nicolò, he found Mary an attractive woman but was mature enough to put aside personal feelings when the situation required – as it certainly did at this time.

Nicolò and Bartoletti started their search for a suitable building in Constantinople for the field hospital. They were advised that the heaviest fighting was likely to be around the Romanus Gate, so found a generously proportioned merchant's house, suitable for conversion, near to the gate. The entrance to the house was wide enough to accommodate stretchers, there were two large rooms at ground level which could be turned into wards, and there was a separate room which could serve as an operating theatre. They visited nearby monasteries, and the monks offered help with nursing, medicine and the provision of long-term care to the seriously wounded.

Over the following weeks, Nicolò and a team of experienced monks and nuns equipped the medical centre with operating tables, beds, storage for medicines and medical instruments. Staff included administrators, nurses and volunteers from the local community. Nicolò organised training days. He knew it would be a shock for many of the volunteers to see battle wounds at close quarters. Nicolò was only too aware that his personal experience was very limited so he engaged the services of an artist to drew pictures of the injuries caused by arrows, swords, clubs, spears and cannon fire as described by more experienced surgeons and nurses. The diagram was cross-referenced to the recommended treatment. His team demonstrated surgical procedures such as stitching wounds, the application of unguents, ointments, honey (a disinfectant and antimicrobial agent), plasters and bandages. Nicolò did his best to encourage staff by assuring them that most battlefield wounds could be successfully patched up, and that patients would make a full recovery provided treatment was given quickly enough.

Nicolò presented his plan for the field hospital at the next meeting of Council. One issue, raised by the Emperor, was that soldiers fighting on the battlements would not be able to leave during the fighting because the access doors to turrets would be locked to prevent troops deserting. Therefore it would not be possible to carry the wounded to the field hospital until the fighting had died down. To get around this problem it was agreed that a small number of medical staff would be posted to the battlements before an attack and remain there until it ended. In this way, the wounded could be given first aid while the fighting continued around them. Afterwards, the wounded would be stretchered to the field hospital. Council approved his plan.

The reunification service in the Church of Santa Sophia was held on the thirteenth of December 1452. The Emperor Constantine and his party, including members of the council, entered through the great bronze doors and crossed the cloisters into the centre of the church where the faithful were gathered. Light from the upper windows in the dome illuminated the scene through clouds of aromatic smoke rising from the hundreds of scented candles lit by the pious. The great mosaic of the mother of Christ holding her son looked down from the dome to protect them. The faithful prayed to her to save themselves, their children and their city in this hour of great peril. The altar was covered with golden chalices filled with hosts of unleavened bread for distribution after the consecration.

The clergy, Orthodox and Latin, entered from behind the altar singing alternate verses in Latin and Greek. The Greeks had no enthusiasm for the union of the churches, profoundly distrusting the Pope of Rome and his claims to infallibility, but they realised that they needed help. The sound of the hymns rose up into the dome. The Papal Legate and Orthodox Patriarch jointly pronounced the words of consecration over the bread and wine. The consecrated hosts were distributed by the clergy to the faithful, who approached the altar in long lines curving and winding across the stone floor. Their feet made a quiet, soothing, shuffling sound. The afternoon light slanted more obliquely from the windows as the afternoon faded. Clouds of perfumed prayers rose from the swinging thuribles. At the end of the service, the Papal Legate and the Patriarch declared the reunification of Catholic and Orthodox faiths to be complete.

The unenthusiastic congregation slowly made its way out of the church as the sun set. Nicolò and Bartoletti walked down the hill from Santa Sophia to the dock. The walk took about half an hour, and they boarded the next ferry. When they disembarked in Galata, they toiled slowly and disconsolately up the steep street to their house where dinner awaited them. They invited Mary Celovic to join them. It was clear to all of them that matters were drawing to a head in a most menacing way.

But on the twenty-sixth of January the city had tangible proof that the reunification service had been worth the effort. Two Genoese galleys, under full sail, rounded the promontory and entered the Golden Horn. The seamen lowered the sails and rowed the last half mile to the wharf by the Gate of Saint John. There they moored. The news of the ships' arrival spread like wildfire through Galata and the city. Citizens turned out to watch. Crowds of people hung over the walls along the Golden Horn. Men, women and children leaned over in great excitement. Here at last were the promised reinforcements who could save the city. Nicolò and Bartoletti hurried across from Galata to join the celebrations. At midday the Emperor Constantine himself came to welcome the ships. The crowds on the walls cheered and clapped.

In the early afternoon the ships started to disgorge their cargo. It was a cargo of inestimable value – seven hundred fighting men fully equipped with armour and personal weapons. They were not ordinary soldiers but mercenaries, whose business was fighting for money and the spoils of war. The soldiers walked down the gangways carrying weapons that glinted in the winter sunshine. Their bearing was arrogant, their faces thin and cruel. They did not acknowledge the cheers from the city walls. There were no smiles. They had come to do a job.

The leader of the mercenaries was Giovanni Giustiniani who had personally funded the venture. He had a formidable reputation for successfully defending besieged cities. The Emperor went to his ship to welcome him. 'We are more than pleased to see you, Giustiniani, and we have great need of your services at this difficult time. We will provide a camp for your men near the Blachernae Palace. Take your men there, settle in, and we will meet tomorrow at Council to discuss how best you can serve us.'

The mercenaries marched off two abreast down the wharf and through the Gate of Saint John. They did not have the smart discipline of the Turkish troops but they were battle-hardened and tough. Constantine felt confident enough to give their leader, Giustiniani, the overall command of the city's land forces.

Report to the Doge
28 February 1453

Your Excellency,

The city rejoiced when seven hundred Genoese mercenaries arrived in late January. They are commanded by Giovanni Giustinani who is known to you. There is no doubt that these troops will play an essential part in defending the city. Unfortunately, their arrival was offset to some extent by the loss of other men who have fled from the city out of fear of the Turks.

I have put in place my plans for medical facilities. Monasteries and convents will supply doctors and nurses and give other assistance. We have done what we can, but I fear it will not be enough given the large forces of the enemy threatening the city. We fear that our medical facilities will be overwhelmed with hundreds, if not thousands, of casualties when the Turks attack.

The enemy is reported to have developed new siege guns which could inflict great damage on the city walls. These cannon are on their way to Constantinople from Adrianople. We await the imminent arrival of the Turkish army with trepidation.

Please confirm that the Venetian fleet is on its way.

Your respectful servant,
Dot. Nicolò Barbaro

7

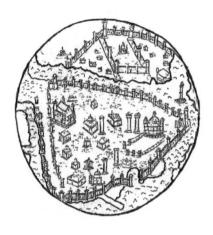

The Siege Begins

t was early April and the Turks had not yet come. It was tempting to think that the danger had gone away. As the weather got warmer, wild flowers and blossom brought cheer to the wooded slopes along the Bosphorus. The north wind blowing from the Black Sea had lost its Russian chill. Spring was coming, but slowly and reluctantly.

On the first Sunday in April, George and Helene Sphrantzes asked Nicolò and Bartoletti to a family lunch. Bartoletti had become a firm favourite with the children to whom he was unfailingly kind and affectionate. As Nicolò was taking his seat at the table, he announced, 'I have started to keep a diary. We live in a time of extraordinary events. What is happening will be forgotten unless someone keeps a record.'

George interposed, 'I myself am writing a history of the Byzantine Empire. However, I am sure that there must be room for another account, if you wish to write one.' He was a noted historian in his own right. In his view, only academics could do justice to recording the past, and he doubted if a Venetian surgeon, competent though he might be in his own field, could understand and explain the significance of the great events taking place in Constantinople.

That spring morning, the family and their guests talked as friends. There were six of them around the table – George and Helene, their children, John and Tamar, and their guests, Nicolò and Bartoletti. The servants placed an abundance of food and wine on the table and served the first course. Then it was up to the diners to help themselves.

The children, John and Tamar, expressed their views forcibly and argued with spirit. Sometimes they had to be quietened down by their parents when they became too animated. In his own childhood, Nicolò had not had the freedom of such cut and thrust in family discussions. Perhaps it was the Greek tradition that ideas and opinions should be challenged and tested, even by young children. It was such a relaxed and enjoyable occasion in the spring sunshine. Lunch was not to be hurried.

But today Nicolò sensed that all was not well. He felt the tension between husband and wife of things unsaid. Helene had on previous occasions confided to Nicolò her wish to leave Constantinople with the children before the siege began. Today she raised the issue again, perhaps emboldened by the presence of strangers.

'Husband, my friends tell me that Captain Davanzo is sailing to the Aegean with families who want to leave. I think we should send the children to Chios to live with my parents until this business is over. The children will be safe there. This could be our last chance.'

George laid his hand on her arm. 'Helene, we have talked of this before. You know that I cannot go while Constantine needs me. He would see my family leaving as a betrayal of our friendship and as setting a bad example to others who cannot escape. In any case, I fear you are too late. Captain Davanzo and his ships sailed two nights ago. They left secretly to avoid the Turkish patrols.'

Helene was shaken to learn that the ships had left. She had placed so much hope on the children escaping. Her eyes filled with tears which ran unchecked down her cheeks and onto the table. She sat with her head bowed and sobbed. It was so unexpected. Nicolò felt embarrassed for her. He had thought Helene a great beauty when he first met her. Now he saw a mother drawn, tired and desperate. She had lost all decorum. Her grief poured out onto the table. John, seeing his mother's distress, got up and walked around to where she was sitting. He put an arm around her shoulders.

'Don't trouble yourself, Mother. I will protect you and Tamar. I will kill a hundred Turks if they dare to come.'

Pulling herself together, his mother said, 'It is I who should protect you, my son. Your father will not let us leave. If we cannot leave, we must stay together. I pray to God that the Turks will not come.'

Lunch finished. The laughter and joy had fled. As Nicolò and Bartoletti walked back to the ferry, they talked of their fear for the future of Constantinople and for the fate of the Sphrantzes family. It was obvious that the children should have been sent to Chios. George was blindly following his master, dragging with him his wife and children.

The Turks did come. In the early morning of the fifth of April 1453, one hour after daybreak, they appeared. The Byzantine lookouts were facing north where the hilly countryside stretched away towards Adrianople. Morning mist clung to the trees on the edge of the forest. The sentries were preparing to stand down when they noticed movement among the thinning trees at the edge of the forest. The Byzantine pickets came running out of the woods heading for the Romanus Gate. They ran like rabbits chased by a fox. Behind them, Turkish cavalry burst out of the trees and, once in the open, drew their scimitars. When they caught up with the fleeing men, the horsemen sliced down onto their defenceless heads and shoulders. A few fortunate ones, those who ran fastest, made it inside the city gate. The less fortunate fell to the ground in full view of watchers on the city wall, their bodies forming a vector pointing to the heart of the city.

The whole of that day the Emperor, together with members of Council and military leaders, watched as the enemy forces emerged from the forests. There seemed to be no end to them. Constantine asked George to keep a tally. The Turks halted that night two and a half miles from the city. They were organised and disciplined, and each cohort knew where it had to make camp. They lit fires and calmly settled in for the night, seemingly confident of a swift victory.

George estimated that more than one hundred thousand Turkish troops arrived that day. Towards evening a final group appeared, led by a figure on a white horse surrounded by a retinue and a bodyguard of Janissaries. They assumed that this must be Sultan Mehmed although he was still too far away for them to be sure. The following day Mehmed, for it had been he, moved half his forces to within a mile of the city walls. The day after, the seventh of April, the Sultan moved most of his men to within a quarter of a mile of the city. The Turkish forces stretched along the full six miles of the land walls. There they made camp in full and menacing view of the besieged citizens.

How could the city defend itself against this overwhelming might? Every man, woman and child had seen them arrive with mounting despair. This was what being under siege meant – fear, terror and certain death if the enemy broke in. They were like the Jews surrounded by Roman armies at the siege of Jerusalem. Christ had warned them. Now they must pay for murdering their Saviour. Would Christ save the Byzantines when he had not saved his own people? Why should he take pity on a people who dedicated themselves to business and the accumulation of wealth?

Constantine understood the people's terror at the overwhelming number of the enemy. He needed to do something to raise their spirits and instil some hope. He ordered the three galleys from the Isle of Tana and two other galleys to leave their anchorage off the Pera and to row to Chinigo Harbour. There a thousand fighting men disembarked, fully armed and in good order, with banners unfurled and led by their officers, who presented themselves to Constantine asking what orders he had for them.

Constantine commanded them, 'Go around the city walls on the landward side, so that the faithless Turks, our enemies, can see the men in such good order and see that there are many fighting men in the city.'

They obeyed his orders and made a good show with music, shouts and banging of swords on shields. This display gave great comfort to the people and caused some surprise among the enemy.

Constantine wanted to know how many fighting men he had at his disposal so he turned to his friend, George Sphrantzes. 'George, I want you to estimate how many soldiers we have. You will need to be discreet for I fear it will be much smaller than the numbers of the enemy.'

George agreed to do a tally. In the next two days he visited all the barracks and encampments in the city. He discussed with the captains of the galleys moored in the harbour the number of crew able and willing to fight. He visited monasteries to count the number of monks ready for battle. When he had finished, he informed Constantine that there were five thousand Greeks and two thousand foreigners, including the recently arrived mercenaries and archers, making a total of seven thousand fighting men. The Ottoman numbers were estimated at well in excess of one hundred thousand fighting men.

Constantine said, 'This is even worse than I expected. Under no circumstances should the people be told or they will lose heart. No amount of marching around the walls can disguise this huge disparity in forces.'

George tried to find some positives. 'Our men have better armour and better weapons. The city walls will be difficult to scale. Our archers will shoot down the enemy as they try to climb up. The walls are one hundred feet high. If any enemy reach the parapets, we will toss them back down. I agree that the numbers are against us, sire, but the city has repelled many enemies in the last thousand years. Pray that God will be on our side.'

The Emperor distributed his limited forces as best he could in consultation with the newly arrived Giustiniani. The bulk of their forces were positioned along the landward walls facing northward towards Adrianople. The weakest part of the defences was at the place where the Lycus River flowed under the walls at the Cressu Gate. This was a good position for an enemy to site cannon and to undertake mining operations. The Emperor kept a group of his most trusted knights around him as a bodyguard. The Venetian bailor moved into the Blachernae Palace to defend it at the weak point where the palace wall joined the city wall. Loukas Notares commanded a small strategic reserve of one hundred cavalry located in the Forum of Theodosis. Genoese archers manned the towers along the land walls where even a small number of bowmen in each tower could do great damage. The monks and a small force of Turkish troops under Dorgano Bey guarded the walls along the seashore and the Golden Horn.

On the ninth of April, the Emperor ordered the deployment of the boom across the entrance to the Golden Horn. The boom was made of large wooden blocks linked together by a metal chain secured at either end in Galata and Eminönü. Ten trading galleys, five from Genoa, three from Candia and one from Ancona, and a single ship supplied by the Emperor, moored along the boom.

The Turkish artillery arrived six days after the infantry. Sultan Mehmed positioned three cannons opposite the Blachernae Palace, three at the Pigi Gate, two at the Cressu Gate and four at the Romanus Gate, including the two enormous siege cannons built by Orbán. Earth banks in front of the guns protected them from Byzantine fire and from raids by skirmishers. Supplies of gunpowder, wadding and shot were stored behind each of the earthworks.

The bombardment began two days later. Nothing could have prepared the people for the deafening noise of the guns. It could take up to an hour to load the larger guns and the timing varied from gun to gun. They fired, therefore, at irregular intervals, but the overall effect was of a linked series of blasts blending into one continuous roar which went on day and night without cessation. For the people of Constantinople the thunderous noise wrecked their sleep and threatened their sanity. The smell of gunpowder filled their lungs with coarse dust, which even the breezes off the Marmora could not dispel. They longed for the bombardment to cease, for a moment of silence, but there was no pause and no silence.

The Turkish objective was to blast away at the walls until they collapsed. Each firing was followed a few seconds later by a thud as the shot hit the walls. After enough blows the facing stonework would fall away clattering down the wall into a pile of broken rubble. The defenders had to repair the damage as quickly as possible to prevent the collapse of whole sections. Every night, the defenders, mostly non-combatants, crept out from gates at the base of the towers to gather up the loose stones. The recovered stones were bound together in nets of rope and fibre which were packed around with earth. The repaired sections proved surprisingly resistant to cannon shot, being softer than the original stone facings and better able to absorb the blows.

But it was dangerous work. The Turks sent out raiding parties to clear the repair crews, and many brave volunteers, mostly old men, women and children, did not return, but repairing the walls was a matter of life or death if the city was to be saved. Why else send women and children to their deaths?

Nicolò tried to dissuade John Sphrantzes, George's son, from going outside, but he and his friends were determined. The young boys felt themselves invincible. They rushed out, ignoring the danger. John would call out to Nicolò, 'Dottore, I will be back before dawn.' Helene and Tamar volunteered at the field hospital each night.

On the twelfth of April, the Turkish fleet of one hundred and forty-five ships arrived at Constantinople. They anchored off the Asian shore, but later moved across the Bosphorus to the European shore. As their ships approached the boom, the crews gave vehement cries and sounded castanets and tambourines. Nicolò was concerned that the loud shouts, the sight of so many galleys and their position so close to the boom would fill the Byzantine sailors and defenders in the city with fear.

The Turks did not press home their attack that day. They moved a little way up the Bosphorus to the Two Columns anchorage off the Pera. There they were so close to the Golden Horn that the Byzantines were forced to post two men on the walls of Galata so that any movement of the Turkish fleet could be reported immediately to the Byzantine naval commander. The risk of an attack by the Turkish fleet at any time of the day or night stretched the nerves of the defenders to breaking point.

On the twentieth of April, four large Genoese galleys carrying supplies and food to the city appeared unexpectedly from the direction of the Princes' Islands. From the Galata Tower, Nicolò and Bartoletti watched the galleys, in a strong southerly wind, driving towards the Golden Horn. They had almost reached the safety of the harbour when the wind died. The ships lay becalmed. The Turkish fleet, seeing their predicament, left the Two Columns to seize the ships. Soon a cluster of Turkish warships surrounded each of the becalmed galleys.

The furious battle lasted for four hours without the Turkish ships being able to board the Genoese galleys. The Genoese fought tenaciously. Archers in the rigging fired arrows down on the enemy. The defenders emptied cauldrons of Greek fire onto the attackers' heads. Any Turk reaching the deck was cut down. In the end there was no clear victory for either side, but the Christians won great honour for the way they defended themselves against such overwhelming odds. When darkness fell, the Byzantines sent out ships to tow the Genoese galleys into the Golden Horn. The battle was fought very close to the shore. The people cheered the Genoese from the walls. Here were four plucky Christian ships defending themselves against a wolf pack of enemy galleys.

Sultan Mehmed rode his horse along the seashore, shouting encouragement. As the battle continued, he grew angrier at the failure of his fleet to capture the four ships. The Sultan's shouts turned into abuse and violent threats. The failure of the Turks was a personal humiliation. Someone must pay the price. The next day the Sultan, with an escort of ten thousand men, rode around the Golden Horn to the Two Columns where the Turkish fleet was anchored. Mehmed summoned Baltaoğlu – the Turkish admiral.

'Traitor to the faith of Mahomet, traitor to me, your master, why were you unable, with all the ships under your command, to capture four Christian ships, when they were an easy fight, being held by a dead calm?'

The admiral pleaded that he had fought fiercely without taking a backward step and begged for mercy, but Mehmed replied, 'Traitor, I will myself cut off your head.'

The admiral was saved by his fellow commanders pleading for his life to be spared. Mehmed relented but stripped him of his command and appointed Hamza in his place. The Sultan then returned to his camp which was opposite the Romanus Gate. Here, the bombardment of the city walls continued ceaselessly. A tower in the city wall was razed along with twenty yards of wall. There were a series of skirmishes led by the Janissaries. It was the first time that the defenders had seen the Janissaries fighting, and they told Constantine that none of them were afraid of death, but the enemy were like wild beasts. When one or two of them were killed, at once more Turks came and took away the dead ones, carrying them on their shoulders as one would a pig without caring how near they came to the city walls. The city's defenders shot at them with guns and crossbows, aiming at the Turk who was carrying away his countryman, and both would fall to the ground dead, and then there came others who took them away rather than suffer the shame of leaving a single Turkish corpse by the walls.

The siege had been going on for three weeks without the Turks being able to enter the city. On the landward side the Turkish forces had not been able to break through the walls, and by sea the Genoese and Venetians had demonstrated their superior seamanship and benefited from the security of a safe anchorage within the Golden Horn.

Mehmed needed a change in his tactics. The Turkish sailors were ordered to clear a route three miles long from the Two Columns, up the hill around Galata and down into the waters of the Golden Horn. The Turks put greased rollers across the roadway. They lifted a number of their smaller boats onto the rollers and dragged them, at night, to the Golden Horn. In a single night they managed to move seventy-two small galleys without the Byzantines being aware of what was happening.

Next day, the Emperor and the people of Constantinople, including Nicolò and Bartoletti, awoke to the fearful realisation that their fleet was vulnerable to attack both from the sea and from within the harbour. There, just below Galata, nestled a veritable fleet of Turkish ships which had not been there when the people of Constantinople went to bed the night before. The young Sultan was proving to be a commander of exceptional imagination and ability. The Byzantines had, once again, been out-thought and out-manoeuvred.

The Emperor called a meeting of his council in the Church of Santa Maria to debate what might be done to counter the new threat. Various options were discussed, but the idea that found most support came from Giacomo Coco, master of the galley from Trabizon. Coco suggested a surprise night attack with fire ships to burn the Turkish boats moored in the Golden Horn. The plan was approved by Council.

The intention was to attack as soon as possible. Two large galleys had their sides padded with sacks of wool and cotton to reduce the impact of cannon balls. The fire ships were to be escorted by armed ships captained by Gabriele Trevisano and Zacaria Grioni and three fast skiffs commanded by Silvestrio Trivixen, Girolamo Morexini and Giacomo Coco. A number of small brigantines were filled with pitch, brushwood and gunpowder to be set alight and sailed towards the Turkish boats. The order was given to be ready for an attack at midnight.

Had they attacked that night, they might well have succeeded, but the attack did not go ahead. The Genoese in Galata got wind of the plan. The Podestà was eager to curry favour with the

Turks to the disadvantage of the Venetians who were to spearhead the attack. The treacherous Podestà sent messengers to inform the Sultan of the plan, and then he suggested to Council that the Genoese join in the attack alongside the Venetians.

'You should not make this attempt alone tonight, but if you wait for one more night, we, the Genoese of Galata, offer our companionship to you for the better burning of their fleet.'

Trevisano and the other masters agreed to postpone the attack. Meanwhile, the Sultan, forewarned, sent a great number of soldiers to protect the Turkish fleet in the Golden Horn. He positioned cannon on the beach and on the other side of the inlet to bombard the fire ships.

The Byzantine attack finally took place on the twenty-eighth of April. Two hours before daybreak, the attackers set out across the Golden Horn towards the Turkish boats. Even then the attack might have succeeded but for the over-enthusiasm of Giacomo Coco, master of the galley of Trabizon, who raced ahead of the other ships. The Turkish cannon opened up and at the second shot hit his galley amidships. The ship sank immediately with the loss of all hands. The other light galleys following behind did not realise what had happened due to the smoke from the cannon. Gabriel Trevisano's galley was also hit but managed to beach. At this setback, the other attacking ships turned back and returned to the protection of the boom. So, the Turks won the battle and the Christians wept bitterly for the unfortunates who drowned.

The Turks captured a number of sailors from the Christian ships. Mehmed decided to make an example of these men who had dared to defy him. They were condemned to death by impalement. The next day fifteen young men were executed on the dockside in full view of the people of Constantinople. Each of the condemned was dragged along the dock to the place where they were to die. Their executioners were in no rush. One by one the youths were thrown down. An executioner drove a pointed wooden stake into each man with a large wooden mallet. Ignoring the victims' screams of agony, the mallets rose and fell driving the stakes up through the soft inner tissue of the stomach and under the victim's rib cage. The executioners then placed the stakes into the holes which had already been prepared. The young men hung there until, by the mercy of God, death released them from their suffering. From the walls of Constantinople there came a deep rumbling of fury and grief. These men had been sons or husbands. It was an act of barbarity intended to strike terror into the people of Constantinople.

Constantine knew the people wanted revenge. He instructed his men to bring up all the Turkish prisoners held in his dungeons. 'Bring up all the enemy prisoners. Hang all two hundred and sixty of them from the towers along the walls – four to each tower. We will match blood for blood.'

The emperor's orders were obeyed. Each tower around the city was decorated with twisting bodies. Nobody pleaded their cause. This was vengeance pure and simple. Now it was total war. Mercy, forgiveness and chivalry died that day.

Report to the Doge:
1 May 1453

Your Excellency,
Yesterday, our sailors tried to launch an attack on the Turkish navy using fire ships, but the plans were leaked to the Sultan by certain treacherous Genoese. Our young men, who were taken

prisoner, paid an appalling price for the Genoese treachery.

The Turks have the city surrounded by many troops and a large fleet. Supplies are not getting through and starvation is a real threat. Our men, women and children fight with great courage but for how much longer can they go on?

The Emperor has dispatched a fast sailing barque to the Aegean with orders to locate the Venetian fleet which was promised to us. If they locate it, they will urge them to come to Constantinople with all dispatch to raise the siege which threatens the very existence of Constantinople and its Christian civilization.

Meanwhile, the Emperor has posted lookouts on the highest tower in the city. They watch for the arrival of the Venetian fleet, as a shepherd tending his sheep, awaits the light of dawn. If reinforcements do not arrive soon, all will be lost and many will die.

Your servant,
Dot. Nicolò Barbaro

8

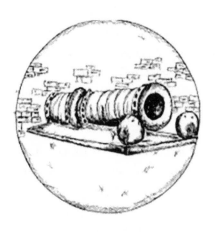

Pounding of the Walls
May 1453

I t had been unremitting. The noise, the shaking of the ancient walls, the fall of masonry, the stench of gunpowder and the cries of men, women and children. The abnormal had become the normal. When will it end, the people asked? The answer: when the city falls or the Turks depart. Will we be alive when all this is over? The answer: God has written each man's name in the book of life, when his life will begin and when it will end. So ask him – when will my life end? Now is the time to pray and to sharpen your swords on whetstones.

The Turkish cannons pounded the walls around the

Romanus Gate. Their smoke drifted over the city walls and over the rooftops of the houses. The areas within range of the guns were desolate, street after street of buildings reduced to rubble with, here and there, a jagged wall or church tower still upright. Destitute children sought safety in cellars at night while during the day they begged passers-by for food. Many had fled their houses by the walls and sought refuge with relatives and friends in the centre of the city.

From the top of the Galata Tower, Nicolò could see the line of Turkish cannon positioned on the heights above the Pera. The Turkish gunners were reloading and he could hear officers shouting orders. Every few minutes, a cannon fired. His eyes followed the trajectory of the shells in the clear sky above the town and their graceful arching down into the Golden Horn where the Byzantine galleys sheltered as close as they could under the town walls.

Nicolò and Bartoletti had settled into a routine. In the morning, they visited the Galata medical practice where Nicolò saw the patients who needed a doctor's attention rather than routine nursing care. In the afternoon, they took the ferry across to Constantinople and walked the three miles to the field hospital near the Romanus Gate. They checked that the stocks of medicine had been replenished and that the nuns had cleaned the operating tables and washed the medical instruments, which were placed by the side of the tables. The nursing sisters prepared fresh medicine and wound treatments each day. For deep wounds, they pounded a red paste of black wine, mineral haematite, nutmeg, white frankincense, gum arabic and dragon's blood. The paste was applied to wounds before the skin was stitched back.

As it grew dark, the two men took up their positions on the walls with the medical orderlies. When an attack ended, any wounded men were moved on stretchers to the field hospital as quickly as possible. Sometimes, Nicolò had to operate throughout the night if casualties were particularly heavy. The wounds he treated varied greatly in type and severity depending on what had caused them, whether arrows, crossbow bolts, splinters of shattered masonry, fragments of cannon shells or close-combat sword and spear thrusts. Each wound had its recommended treatment, but usually his first action, after stemming the flow of blood, was to cut open the flesh and extract any missile fragments. He was aware of the pain he caused the patients but had learned to close his mind to it. He used a scalpel to split open the flesh then folded back the skin to give room to dig about with his fingers to find and remove fragments of metal or stone. He worked as fast as he could, but inevitably the wounded men suffered greatly since there was no effective analgesic. Once the arrowheads and/or other foreign bodies had been removed, the red paste was rubbed into the cavity then the skin was sewn together with fine thread. When the surgery was completed, the nurses bound the wounds with clean bandages. Lastly, the patient was moved into the ward or to a monastery for further treatment.

Late on the morning of the fifth of May, a Genoese galley in the Golden Horn was hit by Turkish gunfire from the Pera, sinking the ship with its valuable cargo of silk, wax and other merchandise to a value of twelve thousand ducats. On the eighth of May, the Emperor called a meeting of the Council of the Twelve to discuss what they should do to protect the galleys. After much debate, Council decided to unload the cargo of the galleys from Tana and to sink them alongside the boom to discourage further attacks by the Turkish fleet.

When the crews of the galleys realised what was planned, they protested vehemently. 'Let us see the man who will take the cargoes from these galleys! We know that where our property is there are our homes also, and we also know that as soon as we have unloaded these galleys and sunk them, at once the Greeks will keep us in their city by force as their slaves, whereas now we are at liberty either to go or to stay. It would be better to stop unloading the galleys and place ourselves under the mercy of our Lord God. So, we have decided to die here in the galleys, which are our homes.'

Council reluctantly agreed that the ships should stay where they were and the cargoes were not unloaded.

The Council met again on the ninth and tenth of May at the Church of Santa Maria of Constantinople. Gabriel Trevixen, captain of two ships, was ordered to take four hundred marines to reinforce the defence of the city walls. Council promoted Captain Aluvixe Diedo to overall command of the ships in the harbour, and he worked diligently to put them into good order and to secure the boom.

On the twelfth of May, Sultan Mehmed launched a determined attack on the city along the landward walls. Fifty thousand troops came right up to the walls near the Blachernae Palace with fierce cries and sounds of castanets and tambourines. Their attack was repelled with flaming arrows and cauldrons of super-heated oil. The defenders were few in number, but they were experienced troops, well armed, protected by superior body armour and desperation. The Christian archers found ready targets as the Turkish soldiers climbed slowly up their shaky ladders towards the battlements. Turks, pierced by arrows, fell backwards onto those climbing up behind them. After three hours of fierce fighting, the Turkish assault slackened and that night the enemy failed to get into the city.

When the direct assaults failed, the Sultan changed tactics. He ordered the Turks to dig a tunnel starting at a point half a mile away from the walls. On the night of the sixteenth of May the noise made by the Turkish miners was detected and reported to the Emperor and Grand Duke Loukas Notares. They sought out men with mining experience among their troops and succeeded in digging a counter-tunnel from which they broke into the Turkish tunnel. The Byzantines threw in fire, burning the wooden roof props and causing the roof to collapse, suffocating and burning many of the Turkish miners. This was a welcome victory. Even so, the Byzantines were afraid that the Turks would emerge from other tunnels to kill and murder them and their families in the night.

The defenders were allowed no respite. Just two days later, as the sun rose, they were shocked to find themselves facing a siege tower positioned just ten paces away from the city walls. The new tower was higher than the battlements so that the Turks could fire down on the Byzantine defenders on the ramparts. The sudden appearance of the siege tower caused panic.

Constantine came with his nobles to see what had happened. He was shocked and afraid. The tower was yet another new Turkish tactic. It was not that siege towers were new. After all, the Romans had used such towers at the siege of Jerusalem, but it was yet another Turkish initiative, like the new cannon and the movement of ships overland, which testified to an efficient organisation, iron discipline and limitless resources. Mehmed was an absolute ruler who had no need to seek the permission of others before acting. He had decided to build and assemble a siege tower in a single night and his orders had been obeyed to the letter.

The bombardment of the great guns continued to bring down stretches of wall. The cannon fire became more effective following a meeting between Mehmed and a Hungarian bombardier, who advised him that cannon fire should be triangulated rather than aimed at a single point. Mehmed took his advice. As a result, the bombardment brought down whole sections of the walls.

The day of the twenty-first of May was thrust and counter-thrust. The sides were probing for weaknesses. Even before the sun rose, the Turkish fleet moved to attack the Christian ships in the harbour, an event witnessed by Nicolò, watching from the Galata Tower, as they hauled up their anchors. He helped raise the alarm so that the whole city was prepared to repel the attack, and each man stood in the place assigned to him by the Emperor. When the Turks heard the tocsin, they realised that the Christians were well prepared so they decided against attacking and their fleet withdrew. At noon another tunnel was discovered at Calgaria near the Emperor's palace, but it was quickly destroyed. The bombardment continued all day as did the repairing of the walls. The defenders were exhausted by these constant attacks.

Mehmed sent an ambassador to Constantine to offer terms for a peaceful resolution of the siege. The Sultan's ambassador offered Constantine land in the Peloponnese, and guaranteed free passage for Constantine and any followers who wished to leave the city, while at the same time promising safety to any citizens who decided to remain. Constantine countered by offering to pay a higher annual tribute and to recognise the right of Mehmed to any castles or territory which he had won. But Constantine would not agree to cede possession of the city, saying, 'Giving you the city depends neither on me nor anyone else as we have all decided to die with our own free will and we shall not consider our lives.' Mehmed's ambassadors returned with this uncompromising answer.

On the Turkish side there were those such as Halil Pasha who advocated calling off the siege, citing the lack of progress to date and the dangers of western help arriving to aid the Christians. However, Halil's arguments were overruled by Mehmed, based on the strong case for pressing forward made by Zaganos Pasha, his fellow pashas and the army leaders.

On the twenty-second of May two further Turkish tunnels were discovered and destroyed. Some Turkish miners were captured. Under torture they gave the locations of all remaining Turkish tunnels before being executed. Nicolò noted in his diary that one of the prophesies of the final days of the Byzantine Empire came to pass. Nicolò had no belief in celestial signs and superstitions but many did believe in them. At the first hour, there appeared a wonderful sign in the sky, which was to tell the worthy Emperor of Constantinople that his proud empire was about to come to an end. After sunset, the moon should have risen in the form of a complete circle, but it rose as if it were no more than a three-day moon, with only a little of it showing, although the air was clear and unclouded, pure as crystal. The moon stayed in this form for about four hours, and gradually increased to a full circle, so that at the sixth hour of the night it was fully formed.

The Emperor, the Christian defenders and the Turks inter-preted this celestial apparition as the fulfilment of the prophecy, 'Constantinople would never fall until the full moon should give a sign'. The sign had been given. It caused great fear among the Christians while the Turks, knowing of the prophecy, made great festivity as they believed that the city would soon to be in their hands.

Constantine still hoped that help was on its way from the west. He ordered a fast brigantine crewed by twelve men to sail to the Aegean to seek the Venetian fleet. They slipped out of the Golden Horn on the night of the third of May with their crew disguised as Turks. The Emperor's orders were to find the Venetian fleet and, when found, to urge the Venetians to come with all speed to the aid of Constantinople. But after days of searching, they could find no trace of it.

Some of the crew argued: 'Brothers, you see clearly that when we left Constantinople a general attack by the Turks was expected at any moment, and you see that the city will be completely overrun by the faithless Turks, because we left it poorly supplied with men of action, and so, my brothers, I say that we should go as quickly as possible to some Christian land because I know very well that by this time the Turks will have captured Constantinople.'

Others argued against this, saying: 'The Emperor has sent us to do this thing, which we have done, and so we wish to return to Constantinople, whether it is in hands of the Turks or of the Christians, and whether we go to death or life, let us go on our way and return to the city as we promised.'

The crew courageously decided to return to Constantinople. Nicolò and Bartoletti watched the ship arrive back early on the twenty-third of May. The Turks mistakenly thought that this lone ship was the vanguard of the Venetian fleet and rowed out to attack it, but when they saw the ship pass through the boom and anchor in the Golden Horn, they returned to their moorings at the Two Columns.

The captain reported to the Emperor Constantine that they had been unable to find the Venetian fleet. Constantine wept in despair. He could not believe that Christ and the Venetians would abandon him. Constantine prayed to the most merciful Lord Jesus Christ, his mother, Saint Mary, and Saint Constantine, founder of the city, to come to their aid.

Another tunnel was located and destroyed. The Turks continued their frenzied attacks on the city walls with cannon fire and gunfire and countless arrows. The Christian forces had a very bad day indeed, but there were festivities in the Turkish camp because they knew that a general assault was soon to be launched.

Report to the Doge:
25 May 1453

Your Excellency,
We await the enemy's final onslaught. It cannot be delayed much longer. There are those who still hope that the attacks of the infidel will be repulsed and victory will be ours. I pray that this may be the case, but I have little hope of such a favourable outcome. I am convinced that we are witnessing the end of the Byzantine Empire.

The passing of this great empire, which has lasted for one thousand years, will inevitably be accompanied by great suffering. As a doctor, I will do my best to alleviate that suffering. We have established a field hospital in the city to give first aid to the wounded, and some of the monasteries have medical facilities, but these will be overwhelmed by the scale of numbers needing help. I fear that no one, men, women or children, will be spared if the Turks break into the city which seems daily more likely.

Perhaps the Venetian fleet will come at last, but we could not find it. Has it even left Venice? Constantine has posted lookouts to search the horizon day and night. We are beginning to lose hope that help will reach us in time.

This may be my final report. If I do not return, please tell my parents that I did my best for the patients in my care and served the Republic of Venice honourably.

Dot. Nicolò Barbaro

9

Encircled by Fire

The air was warm and scented with the smell of spring herbs growing between cobbles. Galata was peaceful. Life in the town carried on despite the distant sound of cannon fire and the whiff of gun smoke drifting over from Constantinople. Here, people smiled and chatted and the street vendors carried on with their businesses. The medical practice, under the management of Mary Celovic, continued with its work.

In the mornings, Nicolò and Bartoletti walked down the street and out through the town gate onto the wharf, along the line of cargo ships, fishing caiques and trading galleys. The choppy waters of the Bosphorus sparkled cheerfully in the sunshine. After lunch on board the *Esmeralda* with Captain Diedo, they took the ferry across to Constantinople to the field hospital, some three miles from the ferry station. They briefed the staff and volunteers at the hospital on the current military situation. Nicolò told them to prepare for a major attack soon. He thanked them for all that they had done. There was still hope that, if the enemy again failed to breach the walls, they might be forced to abandon the siege.

On the battlefield, matters were drawing to a head. On the twenty-sixth and twenty-seventh of May, Sultan Mehmed ordered fires to be lit within the Turkish camp, two fires alongside each tent. On the twenty-sixth the fires burned from sunset until midnight, and on the twenty-seventh they burned all night until dawn. The Turkish soldiers danced and shouted and jumped over the fires like fiends. The flames stretched for three miles along the whole length of the landward walls. It was an inferno. To watchers on the battlements it created the impression that the whole city was sliding down into Hades.

Each night, Emperor Constantine took his post on the battlements fully armoured and ready for battle. He stood in full view of his men and of the enemy. None could doubt his personal courage. The words of the psalm came to mind: 'Though an army encamp against me, my heart shall not fear.' He stood surrounded by his loyal knights – Loukas Notares, George Sphrantzes, Girolamo Minotto, and the captains of the merchant galleys, and faithful chivalric knights Don Francisco, John Dalmata and Theophilis grouped around Constantine for the Emperor's protection. Constantine was the living embodiment of a Roman

Emperor. His helmet was decorated with red feathers in the crest which curved backwards behind his neck. His breastplate was of finely wrought bronze. He wore chain mail over a leather tunic. He carried a Roman sword in his right hand.

As the Ottomans made their fires, they shouted in their Turkish fashion, so that it seemed as if the very skies would split apart. The whole city was in a state of panic, and everyone was in tears and praying to God and to the Virgin Mary that they should escape the fury of the pagans. It is impossible to describe the damage done that day by the cannon to the walls at San Romanus, particularly by the big cannon, so that at this time, the peoples' sufferings were great and they were very fearful.

The defenders stood at their posts throughout the night. The Turkish fires gradually died and, as there was no sign of an imminent attack, Constantine stood down his troops.

On the morning of the twenty-eighth, George Sphrantzes invited Nicolò and Bartoletti to breakfast at his house. They accepted his invitation once the wounded had been patched up in the field hospital, and after the monks had moved those needing longer-term care to the monasteries. Over a simple meal of bread, cheese and olives, they agreed that, in the event of the Turks breaking into the city, their first duty must be to ensure that Helene and the children were safe. Bartoletti was asked to escort them to the Church of the Holy Apostles. The abbot had agreed to shelter the family for the three days during which the Turkish troops would be free to pillage. After three days, they should be able to leave their hiding place and either escape from the city or formally surrender themselves to a Turkish officer. George instructed Helene, 'Tell the officer that you are a relative of the Emperor Constantine and that I am known to Sultan

Mehmed. Assure the officer that I will reward him generously for his protection and will pay the ransom.'

Breakfast was over. Nicolò and Bartoletti bade farewell to the family. All embraced, and the children opened their arms and put them around Nicolò and Bartoletti as if to stop them from leaving. Everyone realised, even the children, that this might be the last time they would meet. The Byzantine world, the world as they knew it, was passing away. No one could be sure what the morning would bring.

'Bartoletti, the children trust you. Keep them safe,' Nicolò urged.

It was now late morning on the twenty-eighth of May. The Turkish trumpets could be heard summoning commanders to prepare for battle. Last night their men had carried two thousand siege ladders over the defensive ditches to the city walls. In addition, they brought up hurdles to protect their troops against arrows as they raised the ladders against the walls. During the day, the Turks moved troops, unit by unit, to their designated positions. Everything was ordered and well planned.

Sultan Mehmed exhorted his troops, 'Children of Mahomet, be of good cheer. Tomorrow we shall have so many Christians in our hands that we shall sell them into slavery at two for a ducat, and we shall have such riches of gold, and from the beards of the Greeks we shall make leashes to tie up our dogs, and their wives and their sons shall be slaves. Be ready to die with a stout heart for the love of our Mahomet.'

The Turks danced and shouted in anticipation of victory. They were angry at the incessant blows from rocks and Greek fire thrown down on their heads. They had buried many comrades. Sensing that victory was within their grasp, they thirsted for revenge. When all was done and the Sultan had given his final orders, he returned to his tent which was half a mile from the Romanus Gate. There he made merry with his admiral and other officers, and they all got drunk together according to their custom. The sounds of their revelry carried to the defenders on the battlements.

While the Sultan relaxed, the Byzantines continued to quarrel amongst themselves. The Christians made seven cartloads of defensive shields, called mantelets, to put on the battlements on the landward side. When these mantelets had been made, they were brought to the square in front of Santa Sophia. The bailor ordered the Greeks to carry them at once to the walls. But the Greeks refused to do so unless they were paid, and there was an argument that evening because the Venetians were willing to pay those who carried them, but the Genoese did not want to pay. When, finally, the mantelets were taken to the walls, it was dark and they could not be put in position before the attack.

Morale was further eroded by the fulfilment of the prophecies of the final days of Byzantium. The prophecies predicted that the conqueror would come from the direction of Anatolia, that the moon would give a sign in the sky and that the last emperor would bear the name of Constantine and that his mother would be called Helen. All these things having come to pass, the people feared God had withdrawn his favour from the city. Nicolò prided himself on being a modern man. He was a man of science and learning and had no time for such superstitions which were a throwback to the dark ages. Be that as it may, the great majority of the people believed in prophecies and feared their fulfilment.

In the late afternoon, Helene and her two children walked with their friends and neighbours to Santa Sophia along the

Roman road past the Church of the Holy Apostles, the Roman aqueduct, through the forums of Theodosius and Constantine and the Hippodrome. As they approached Santa Sophia, they could hear the sound of hymns and the chanting of priests. It must be the penitential procession which had started out early in the morning to circle the city to ask God's forgiveness for their sins. The procession had taken several hours because of the distance, the unevenness of the road and the frequent stops for prayer. Four monks at the front of the procession held a golden tasselled canopy above the sacred icons. At one particularly difficult section of the path, near the Church of Saint George, the table on which the icons were being carried tilted sideways, spilling them onto the ground, damaging some of them. The groan emitted by the pilgrims testified to their deep distress that this accident was yet another sign of God's disfavour. The procession finally passed through the great bronze doors of Santa Sophia. The sound of their hymns and chanting died away. As Helene and the children walked in with the other pilgrims, she saw her husband on the opposite side of the church in the company of Constantine. The Emperor in his penitential robes had been among the last to enter. The church was full. The air was unpleasantly stuffy.

The order of service was that of night prayers. It started with the confession of sins followed by the chanting of a psalm, including the verse:

> From evil dreams defend our sight,
> From fears and terrors of the night
> Tread under foot our deadly foe.

Following the psalm, the priest read from the gospels the

words of Christ and then the words of the Nunc Dimittis. Then the cardinal offered a last prayer:

> Abide with us, Lord Jesus,
> For the night is at hand
> And the day is now past.

The service ended as the daylight faded. The congregation made its way out of the church quietly and soberly. In the church they had felt safe and protected from the evil lurking over the city, but their exultation dissipated in the cold night air. They searched for family and friends, here and there, a familiar face, a recognisable gait, a child's voice echoing across the square. Small groups of families, friends and neighbours coalesced and moved together up the side streets until gradually the sound of human voices faded and they were gone.

A final group exited the great bronze doors. They gathered round the commanding figure of Emperor Constantine. Nicolò watched the Emperor Constantine and George Sphrantzes as they stood side by side outside the church. It was clear that George had chosen loyalty to his Emperor over loyalty to his wife and family. Perhaps, he thought, the two friends loved one another more than they loved their wives and children.

Helene wrote in her diary, 'I begged my husband to let us leave with the other families, but he said it would be an act of betrayal to his friend Constantine. What father would put his own children in such peril? I watched him as he left church. He has become such a bookish man with his rounded shoulders and bald spot. Let him go with his precious Constantine and leave us here to our fate.'

Bartoletti walked Helene and the children to their house while Nicolò made his way directly to the field hospital. The sky above the city was clear and cold and filled with stars. The Milky Way provided them with enough light to make their way back along the Middle Road through the Roman and Greek ruins and through the deep shadows under the arches of the aqueduct. They turned right off the Middle Road near the Church of the Holy Apostles and arrived at the Sphrantzes' home after an hour.

Constantine, whatever his fears, had the courage to lead his people. He addressed his men outside Santa Sophia:

'My friends, the great assault is about to begin. A man should always be ready to die for his faith, for his country, his family or his sovereign. Now we must be prepared to die for all four. Constantinople has been a city of glorious achievements and noble tradition for over a thousand years. The treacherous Sultan has declared war in order to destroy the True Faith and to put his false prophet into the seat of Christ. You are the descendants of ancient Greece and Rome, so be worthy of your ancestors. I thank all of you who have come to our aid from Italy and trust you to fight to the end. Do not fear the vast numbers of the enemy nor their fires nor their shouting which they do to make us afraid. Let your spirits be high, be brave and steadfast. I am prepared to die for my faith, my city and my people. With God's help, we will be victorious.'

All present rose when he finished his speech. They pledged to serve him, even to giving their own lives. Constantine walked up to each man asking forgiveness if he had given offence in any way. He embraced all, and then they turned to their neighbours. The men embraced those around them and bade farewell.

It was well past midnight and about three hours before

dawn. The night drew slowly onwards. Still there was no sign of imminent attack. In the silence the Byzantines began to speculate that the enemy had pulled back or postponed that night's attack. Then, unexpectedly, shockingly, out of the silence of the night, came the urgent ringing of a solitary bell. It was the tocsin – an attack was about to start. The bell was joined by bells from other churches until their ringing was loud enough to wake the dead. Fear gripped the hearts and stomachs of every person in Constantinople. Those who had been resting struggled up from their beds. Those already in position on the battlements checked their weapons. The nurses at the field hospital prepared to receive the wounded.

Now they could hear the enemy – the rumble of siege engines, the dragging of ladders into position and the sound of thousands of feet moving over rough ground. The cannon opened up again. The sound of castanets, horns and trumpets started below the walls. The shouts of the enemy soldiers grew nearer. It seemed as if some great slavering beast searching for prey was dragging itself slowly but inexorably towards the city.

Report to the Doge:
29 May 1453

Your Excellency,
I am writing this from the battlements of Constantinople. The Turks are just about to launch their attack. They are determined to capture the city tonight. I am not sure how many of us will survive but hope we give a good account of ourselves. I can see near me the Emperor bravely leading his soldiers.
Bartoletti and I will continue to help the wounded at the

field hospital. There are brave volunteers working there who help despite the danger. We will fight as long as possible, but I fear that the enemy will break into the city tonight.

It is too late to send help. The city is about to be lost to the infidel Sultan. May God have mercy on everyone in Constantinople tonight.

Your servant,
Nicolò Barbaro

10

Fall of Constantinople
30 May 1453

he hour had come. It was still dark, three hours before dawn. Sultan Mehmed left his tent dressed in his finest armour and mounted his white charger. He had given orders to the commanders of the army, the fleet and the artillery, and promised them riches beyond their wildest imaginings if they secured victory. He had planned for this moment since boyhood. Now the prize was within his grasp and failure was not to be contemplated. By daybreak he must possess the city.

The Sultan issued commands to his men, whom he had

divided into three waves of approximately fifty thousand each. The Byzantines heard, rather than saw, the Turkish forces moving to the base of the wall ready for the attack.

The first wave were the bashi-bazouks. These troops were men taken prisoner in wars in the Balkans, Hungary, Germany and Italy. They were not well trained or armed compared to the mercenaries defending the city, but the objective of the first wave was to soften up and exhaust the defenders. They crossed the ditches, shouting and urging one another on, and manoeuvring the makeshift ladders upright against the walls which stretched above them into the night sky. The bashi-bazouks climbed the ladders holding onto the rungs with one hand and their swords and spears in the other. The defenders pushed away the ladders causing many attackers to fall to their deaths. The Byzantines dropped heavy stones onto their heads and the archers, hiding behind the arrow slits in the towers, shot at them with longbows and crossbows. The arrows and bolts sometimes passed through the bodies of more than one attacker, pinning them together in a ghastly embrace as they fell. The first wave continued to press their attack for two hours, but Turkish casualties were heavy and the attack began to waver, with some of the attackers turning back, hoping to escape. But there could be no escape. A line of Janissaries was positioned behind them with instructions to kill any who showed cowardice. The Janissaries cut down the deserters and threw their bodies into the ditch. The defenders saw the Turks fall back. They had driven off the first attack. Constantine came to congratulate and encourage them. Nicolò moved the wounded from the battlements to the field hospital during the pause in the fighting and stayed there to operate on the wounded.

The defenders hoped for more time to recover before the next assault, but Mehmed gave them no time to rest. He ordered the second wave of fifty thousand men into the attack immediately. It consisted of Anatolian Turks from Vizier Ishak's army. They were well armoured and trained. This mass of men descended into the valley of the Lycus River by the Gate of San Romanus and renewed the attack, aided by cannons firing from the banks of the river. After another hour of ferocious fighting their attack too faltered. At this moment, Orbán's great cannon brought down a section of the wall. The collapse of the wall opened a gap through which three hundred of the Anatolians charged. The situation was critical but the Emperor rallied the defenders. They drove the enemy back outside the walls in hand-to-hand fighting and the danger was averted. The Sultan, seeing what was happening, withdrew the Anatolians. However, his tactic of continuous fighting was exhausting the defenders and there was no time to move any more of the wounded to the field hospital.

It was time for the third and final wave. Mehmed ordered the Janissaries into battle. They were his crack troops and his last throw of the dice. They moved forward, led by the army commanders with the Sultan close behind urging them on. The defenders on the walls were very weary after having fought off the first and second waves, while the Janissaries were eager and fresh for the battle. With the loud cries which they uttered on the field, they spread fear through the city and took away the residents' courage with their shouting and noise. The wretched citizens felt themselves to have been taken already and decided to sound the tocsin through the whole city and sounded it at all the posts on the walls, all crying at the top of their voices, 'Mercy! Mercy! God send help from Heaven to this empire of Constantine, so that a pagan people may not rule over the empire.' All through the city, women and men fell to their knees in prayer.

The climax came an hour before daybreak. The Sultan ordered the great cannon to be fired once again and its shot destroyed a section of the repaired wall. Mehmed ordered the Janissaries to renew their attack. It was his last throw. If they failed, he would have to admit defeat as his father had done thirty years earlier. The Janissaries were fanatically loyal to the Sultan for, as little more than boys, they had been taken away from families to serve the Turkish Sultan. The Sultan had promised them that if they took the City they would be allowed three days to plunder and pillage the legendary riches of Constantinople.

The great cannon roared again. Its brought down a stretch of the wall near the San Romanus Gate. The walls collapsed with a sound like an avalanche in a mountain pass. A determined Turkish attack now would penetrate the city's defences before the defenders could repair the damage. Mehmed gave the defenders no chance to recover, but, riding at the head of his troops, he urged the Janissaries up the ruins. He taunted the Christians: 'Now, where is your God?'

It was the ultimate challenge. Both sides believed it was God who decided matters of life and death and the fate of empires. Was this to be the end of the Byzantine Empire? Was this to be the overthrow of an old but tired regime and its replacement to be a new more powerful and energetic Turkish Empire? God must decide.

The Janissaries charged forward, led by the giant, Ulubath Hasan, whom none could best in single combat. He led his men over the piles of masonry, cutting down any man brave enough to stand in his way. He succeeded in driving the defenders away from the walls. The fighting was ferocious and man to man, using short swords and spears. Many died without knowing who killed them. It was a dangerous moment, but the Emperor Constantine saw the danger and rallied his men. Together they drove the Turkish enemy back over the barbican and back down the ruined walls. Hasan was killed as he retreated down the rubble.

Two incidents were destined to change the outcome. Firstly, the Turks discovered an unlocked door at the base of the Kerkoporta tower. Some thirty Turks entered the tower through the open door, ran up the stone steps and raised the Turkish flag at the top of the turret. They were soon driven out but the damage was done. The Turkish flag was clearly visible. A cry arose, 'The Turks are in the city!'

A second incident weakened the defenders' resolve even more. Guistiniani, the army commander, was wounded when an arrow pierced his lower leg. The pain was intense for the arrow was deeply embedded. He ordered his men to carry him back to his ship for treatment, but no one could leave the battlements because the doors to the street were locked. Guistiniani begged Constantine to let him go, assuring him that he would return to his post.

Constantine replied, 'Stay at your post just a little longer and we will repel the enemy. One more counter-attack should be enough to secure victory. After that we will treat your wound.'

Guistiniani continued to press Constantine, saying that he needed urgent treatment. Worn down by his pleas, Constantine allowed him to leave, much against his better judgement. It was an act of kindness which was to cost the Christians dear. Guistiniani's men unlocked the gate and stretchered their leader down from the battlements and took the road towards the harbour.

The effect was catastrophic. The soldiers saw their leader abandon his post. They changed in that moment from an effective fighting force capable of resisting the attacks of the enemy into a rabble of desperately frightened men shouting, 'The Turks have got into the city!' The gates were too narrow for the numbers trying to escape. They fought and struggled to get through and many were crushed and injured. A number fell into the ditch between the battlements and the walls and could not climb out. These men were picked off by Turkish archers.

Bartoletti saw what was happening. From his long experience of war he knew that the Turks would soon break through. He hurried from the tower. In his haste, he missed his footing, crashing against the stone walls of the staircase. His body armour scraped against the wall and helped to steady him. He exited the tower into a narrow street. It was still dark, although in the east the sky was lightening.

He heard frightened cries. Groups of men ran down the cobbled streets leading from the palace. They rushed past him in panic. Where were they going? Perhaps they were going to their homes to defend their families. Bartoletti knew where his duty lay. He had promised Nicolò's father that he would get his son home safely. They must leave the doomed city immediately. There were galleys in the harbour, but they would not wait long and the harbour was three miles away. It would take them at least an hour and a half to get there. They must leave now.

He headed for the field hospital. As he entered, stretcher bearers pushed past him shouting at him to get out of the way. They banged the stretcher against the doorpost and the wounded man gave a scream of pain. The wounded lay in orderly rows. The nuns and brothers from the Chora Monastery administered treatment as best they could, but the seriously wounded needed surgery and Nicolò was the only doctor qualified to perform such operations.

At the far end of the ward, he could see his master amputating the left leg of one of the wounded. Two orderlies held the soldier down. The lower leg below the knee came away when he cut through the bone. Nicolò handed the severed limb to an assistant who threw it into a box of body parts. The patient's stump bled copiously despite the tourniquet around his thigh. It looked a hopeless case. Nicolò was moving on to the next patient as Bartoletti reached him.

'Sir, we must leave. The Turks are in the city. They could be here at any moment'.

Nicolò looked up. 'I cannot leave my patients.'

'You must come with me, master. The Turks will surely kill the wounded when they arrive. They will kill you as well if you stay. There is nothing more you can do here. The monks will look after them. I promised your father that I would get you home.'

Bartoletti turned his master away from the operating table and pushed him unceremoniously out of the hospital. On their way out they passed between the lines of stretchers. A patient called out, 'Doctor, give me something to ease the pain.' They hurried past and out of the hospital into the street. The night air felt deathly cold after the clammy heat and smells of the field hospital and Nicolò began to shiver. Was it just the cold or was it incipient terror of the approaching enemy? The noise of battle echoed up and down the streets, getting closer all the time. Cannon blasts shook the buildings. From the direction of the Romanus Gate, they heard the screams of men being butchered. A desperate urge to run away took hold of him. The enemy would be here at any moment.

11

Flight from the City

30 May 1453

artoletti hurried his master out of the hospital. At the first crossroads, they turned to the right, past the Monastery of Christ Pantocrator onto the Middle Road which led directly to the Church of Santa Sophia. They stopped briefly at the Church of the Holy Apostles where Helene and the children had taken refuge. There was not a single light visible in any of the monastery's many windows. The monks were either asleep or had gone into hiding. The noise of Bartoletti's knocking echoed along the stone corridors, past the monks' cells and into the empty chapel where incense from night prayers was

still smouldering. Just as they were about to give up, a monk in a black habit slid back the grille in the door. His eyes were full of fear. They asked him if the Sphrantzes family were safe. The brother assured him that the family were well hidden. He would not open the door but quickly shut the grille with a grating sound and the frightened eyes disappeared. Leaving the church, they hurried on down the Middle Road. It was almost daylight now. The noise and smell of battle diminished. Crossing the Forum of Theodosius, they could smell the scent of spring flowers growing wild among the fallen stones of forgotten civilizations. A small group of old women were waiting for morning Mass outside Santa Sophia. The two friends hurried past after warning them that the Turks had broken into the city. The two men ran on down the hill to the harbour where there were ten Christian ships along the boom. Early that morning, they learned later, the Turkish fleet had sailed from the Two Columns anchorage below the Pera to attack the Byzantine ships, but on seeing that the Christian sailors were ready for battle they had headed instead across the mouth of the Golden Horn to Constantinople and moored along the sea walls outside the Giudecca Quarter. The Turkish sailors disembarked, leaving their ships unguarded while they rushed into the city to secure their share of the plunder. The preoccupation of the Turkish sailors gave the Christian boats the chance to escape later in the day.

Many were witnesses to the awful events of that morning: 'Waves of Turkish troops went rushing about the city and anyone they found they put to the scimitar, women and men, old and young, of any condition. This butchery lasted from sunrise, when the Turks entered the city, until midday, and anyone whom they found was killed by the scimitar in their rage. They sought out the monasteries, and all the nuns were led to their fleet and ravished and abused, and then sold at auction for slaves throughout Turkey, and all the young women were raped and then sold for whatever they would fetch. The Turks made great slaughter through the city. The blood flowed like rainwater in the gutters after a sudden storm, and the corpses of Turks and Christians were thrown into the Marmora where they floated out to sea like melons along a canal.'

Captain Aluvixe Diedo, the officer in command of the Christian ships in the Golden Horn, sought the advice of the Podestà as to what he should do. Should the fleet fight on or escape while it had the chance? The Podestà, mindful of the need to curry favour with the victorious Sultan, sent a messenger to Mehmed to seek his advice. The treacherous Podestà then closed the town gates of Galata and held Diedo, Bartoletti and Nicolò prisoner. He intended to hand them over to the Turks or to sell them. They realised, too late, the full extent of the Podestà's collaboration with the Turks.

They despaired of escape but God did not wish them to perish. One hour later, the Podestà entered the room where they were being held. 'Follow me,' he ordered. They followed him down the stairs and through a door into a side street. There a young man guided them to the town gate. Passing through the gate, they found themselves on the wharf close to the merchant galleys. The crews were making ready to put to sea. They could only guess as to why the Podestà had decided to release them. Perhaps he feared God's retribution more than he feared the anger of the Sultan. The fugitives hurried along the wharf towards Captain Diedo's ship which was preparing to cast off.

'Make haste,' Diedo shouted, for he had seen a number of Genoese guards coming out of the city gate looking for the escaping prisoners. Nicolò ran up the gangway onto the deck well ahead of Bartoletti. 'Welcome on board, doctor,' said Captain Diedo. 'We have a wounded man below. Could you come to look at him?'

'Yes, I will come as soon as I have my instruments. Bartoletti has them with him. He will be here in a moment.'

Nicolò turned to look for his man. He could see Bartoletti on the wharf still some distance away and struggling under the weight of the medical chest. 'Get a move on,' he shouted. At that moment, the Genoese guards, alerted by Nicolò's shouting, spotted Bartoletti and recognised him as one of the prisoners. They broke into a run, shouting for him to stop, but Bartoletti did not see them coming. When he was almost at the gangway, he heard them behind him. He stopped, turned around and, realising the danger, he threw down the chest and drew his sword, raising his shield to ward off their blows. He killed the first two guards as they ran at him. But they had not come alone. Another six guards charged forward.

Nicolò realised what was happening. If he acted now he might yet save Bartoletti, but he hesitated. He put down his baggage and loosened his sword. He knew that he should rush down the gangplank to rescue his friend, who was in sore need of help, but he was rooted to the spot. If he charged down and attacked the assailants, they might well back off, and yet he did not move. He could not move. The guards had surrounded his friend. A man behind the old soldier struck with a downward thrust of his sword just below the neck. Bartoletti staggered under the blow dropping to his knees. The other guards seized their opportunity with cruel blows and spear thrusts. The veteran warrior tried once more to rise to his feet. This time he could not get up. His attackers drew back in a circle around the wounded man like hounds around an exhausted fox which they had run to ground. Finally, a guard thrust his spear under his rib cage, piercing his heart.

Bartoletti lay dead just a few feet from Nicolò. The Genoese guards kicked the corpse to make sure it was lifeless, then stripped off the armour and took the weapons. Two men seized the legs and arms and swung Bartoletti's body into the sea, followed by the medicine chest. Nicolò watched as the man and the chest sank from sight. A minute before his friend had been alive. Now he was dead. It was so shocking that Nicolò could not take it in. He stared into the black water where the body was disappearing into the darkness.

The galley cast off and clear water opened up between the ship and the dock. The crew rowed until the ship was past the boom, and joined the other Christian boats at the head of the Golden Horn. Over to port they could see the Turkish galleys moored along the city walls. The Christian ships expected the Turks to attack them to block their escape into the Marmara. But God was on their side. The Turkish ships were empty, their crews having abandoned their vessels and entered the city. The Christian ships stayed at anchor for a further two hours to rescue any troops and families who managed to reach the harbour. By midday they deemed it unwise to stay longer. Turkish flags flew from every roof in the city. They hoisted sail in the steady ten-knot north wind and sailed away from Constantinople past the Princes' Islands and up the Sea of Marmora towards the Dardanelles.

Nicolò took up station in the bows. He could see the landward walls on which he had so recently stood and the Gate of San Romanus, scene of the most bitter fighting but now a broken ruin. The city walls were badly damaged and in places flattened. The guns had ceased firing, but there were drifting remnants of cannon smoke above the city. The noise of the siege had died away and it was strangely quiet after the battle. He wondered what was happening. He could see no one moving from where he stood. Where were the people? Hiding? Were the Sphrantzes family safe? What had happened to the patients at the field hospital? What would happen to Mary Celovic and his staff in Galata? He turned to ask Bartoletti, but he was not there, and then he remembered, with horror, that his friend was just one more corpse bobbing in the water among the hundreds of others. A sense of shame at his own cowardice overwhelmed him – he could have saved his friend's life but had failed him when he was most in need of help. There could be no forgiveness nor any hope of redemption – not now, not ever.

Their ship was sailing away from it all. The fate of Constantinople and his friends was no longer in his hands. The galley ploughed its determined way through the unclean sea with the help of the currents and the north wind. The prow bumped corpses out of its way. The further they sailed from the shore the fewer corpses there were. They passed close to the Princes' Islands where the cliffs plunged vertically into pristine waters. Two young boys were swimming off the rocks and waved as the ship sailed past them. Nicolò stared down into the depths. The daylight reached twenty metres down but beyond that there was only darkness. "No sudden gusty winds could ever pierce them nor could the sun's sharp rays invade their depths" to quote the Odessey. Each hour they sailed brought them closer to safety. During the night they passed through the Dardanelles and, as the sun rose, they found themselves alone and safe in the welcoming Aegean Sea.

12

Vengeance is Mine
June 1453

hen all resistance had ceased, Sultan Mehmed entered the city through the Romanus Gate, surrounded by a jubilant crowd of pashas, Janissaries, military commanders and imams with a host of red Turkish banners swirling above their heads. Mehmed's helmet, with its white plume, caught the sunlight as did his armour inlaid with gold. This man on his white war horse might have been Genghis Khan or a Roman emperor so splendid did he look. A great line of troops stretched away behind him down the rubble of the city wall, all of them eager to share the moment of

triumph. The soldiers cheered and chanted verses from the Koran to celebrate the defeat of Christendom. The Sultan's horse picked its way delicately between the bodies of the fallen as if to avoid adding to their sufferings. Some of the corpses seemed to stretch out their arms to pick up the scimitars which lay just out of their reach.

A Roman emperor would have been impressed and gratified by his reception, but Mehmed was not content. He had much to do to consolidate and secure his new capital. His immediate concern was to find the body of the Emperor Constantine, since only if Constantine was dead could the Sultan feel secure. He ordered an immediate search to find the Emperor's body, with a financial reward as an incentive. The eager searchers pulled apart bodies intertwined in life-and-death struggles. Bodies lay in heaps on the battlements and below the walls. The Emperor could not be found among the bloodied and disfigured remains. The searchers resorted to washing the faces of the dead, but still he could not be found. In the end it was his shoes that gave him away. The shoes on one of the corpses bore the insignia of the Byzantine Emperor. The Emperor's body was lifted up, carried down from the walls and laid at Mehmed's feet. Witnesses who had met Constantine testified that this was indeed the Emperor. His decapitated body was buried with full military honours as befitted an emperor and a brave warrior. The skull was stuffed with straw and carried to other eastern rulers to prove that the Byzantine Empire had been overthrown and that Mehmed was the conqueror and the undisputed leader of the Islamic world.

The Sultan's next step was to decide the fate of certain important Byzantine captives. He set up a court in the Hippodrome amid the dust of the chariot tracks and broken columns. The first to plead for his life was the Grand Duke Loukas Notares. He prostrated himself before the Sultan expecting to buy freedom for himself and his family and, hopefully, to be appointed to a leading position in the new Turkish state. He presented the Sultan with a huge treasure of pearls, precious stones and gems worthy of a royal prince, saying, 'I have guarded this treasure for the beginning of your reign. Accept it, I beg you, as my personal gift. I am now your liege man.'

Notares was accustomed to buying his way out of difficult situations. He was shocked by the Sultan's response.

'Inhuman dog, you possessed all this wealth and denied it to your lord, the Emperor, and to your native city. Why did you not offer this treasure to me before this war started? You could have been my ally. As things stand, God has granted me your treasure anyway.'

The Sultan arrested Notares. The next day he questioned him again as to why he had not used his treasure to defend the city, and why he had not advised the Emperor to accept the Sultan's offer to surrender the city in exchange for peace and a new kingdom. The Grand Duke replied that the Venetians and Genoese were to blame for encouraging the Emperor to think that help was on its way.

Mehmed did not offer Notares a post in the new administration, but he kept the treasure for himself and ordered Notares to send his two sons to his camp. Mehmed's sexual appetite for young boys was widely rumoured. It was an impossible demand to make of any father, and the Grand Duke did not comply. The following morning, the Black Aga, eunuch to the Sultan, came to collect the young men. They refused to go with him. The eunuch arrested the boys and their father and put them before the Sultan. Mehmed ordered that the young men be beheaded in front of their father. After they were dead, Notares was beheaded in his turn.

The execution of other Byzantine nobles followed, including the Venetian bailor, Girolamo Minotto, and his son, the Catalan consul and his two sons. Others escaped their fate by bribing the Vizier Zaganos Pasha who interceded with Mehmed on their behalf. The Podestà of Galata was executed, even though he had leaked the Byzantine plans to Mehmed. Halil Pasha, despite his age, seniority and years of service, was imprisoned and executed a few days later. His fault was to have urged the Sultan to make peace before the final assault. The success of the siege was proof that he had given poor advice. The eunuchs visited him early one morning and strangled him with their bowstrings.

The Sultan had given strict orders that buildings must not be harmed and were not part of the general licence to plunder. He passed a Turkish soldier near Santa Sophia extracting gold tesserae from a mosaic. An angry Mehmed drew his scimitar and, with one downward sweep of the razor-sharp blade, cut the man open from shoulder to chest, with the words, 'Did I not make it clear that the buildings belonged to me?'

The Sultan had taken the city but could not disguise his disappointment at its impoverished and rundown state saying: 'What a town this was and we have allowed it to be destroyed.'

Now there was no one left to kill. The search for hidden valuables continued, but already the troops were weighed down with booty which they carried down to the ships anchored by the city walls. There were lines of chained captives, mostly women and children being marched away from their homes and out of the city into holding camps in the defensive ditches. That evening, at the doors of Santa Sophia, the Sultan ordered that the killing and looting cease and the victorious troops return to their camps outside the walls. The day had been a triumph and fulfilled all of the Sultan's ambitions.

On the third day after the city fell, the Sultan held a great and joyful triumph and celebration. Mehmed used the occasion to start healing wounds. He proclaimed that citizens of all ages who had managed to escape should leave their hiding places and come out into the open where they would suffer no harm. He guaranteed that former residents returning to Constantinople would have their houses and property returned to them, and they would be treated according to their rank. Indeed, the Sultan had been shocked to find how few were the number of inhabitants when the city fell. The city was a desolate wilderness. The destruction caused by the Turkish cannons added areas of desolation to empty villages, deserted houses and neglected gardens. The fabled treasures of Byzantium and its works of art and antiquities were nowhere to be found. Even before the present siege, the city had not recovered from the visitation of the Black Death in 1350, which had left a third of the population dead, nor from its brutal occupation by soldiers of the Fourth Crusade in 1204. The Frankish soldiers of the Fourth Crusade had looted the city of its treasures, including the four bronze horses shipped to Saint Mark's in Venice.

The Sultan wanted to build a prosperous city as his capital of the Turkish Empire. The capture of Constantinople had been a triumph, but it was only the first step, and Mehmed wanted to restore it to its former glory. To achieve this, he needed the skills of its former residents. He took immediate steps to encourage them to believe that they could have a worthwhile stake in the new Constantinople. Mehmed appointed George Scholaris as Greek Orthodox Patriarch and officiated at his inauguration. He confirmed Moshe Capsal as Chief Rabbi and a member of his Imperial Council. He took a very pragmatic approach. The Christians and Jews had the skills and expertise which the city badly needed, so he drew up a new trading agreement with Venice which included the right for Venice to appoint an ambassador to Constantinople. The Sultan proved himself to be a skilful politician. He took these steps soon after capturing the city to avoid further undermining the prosperity of Constantinople as he began its restoration to former greatness.

13

Return to Venice
June–July 1453

icolò scanned the horizon, but the sea was empty of Turkish warships. During the night, the crew had rowed with muffled oars through the Dardanelles, a dangerous strait, long and narrow with strong currents. No enemy galleys or cannon from shore had challenged their passage, so perhaps the Turkish fleet was too busy plundering Constantinople to be bothered with their small convoy. The canvas sails groaned and cracked in the strong wind and the galley, like an old dog glad to be let out, shook off the choppy waters as it ploughed its way between the islands of the Aegean.

But Nicolò was not at peace. In his mind, he constantly re-examined his failures. In his panic he had abandoned the wounded patients in the field hospital with only the religious brothers and sisters to protect them and, yes, he had deserted his patients knowing that none of them could expect any mercy at the hands of the victors. He had not even given a wounded man medicine to ease his pain. He had fled to save his own life despite saying that he would never do such a thing. He had not made sure that Mary Celovic was safely with the Franciscan sisters. Worst of all, he had not fought to save his Bartoletti. No, he had cowered on deck and watched the brutal guards beat, kick and plunge their swords into his friend. They had killed him and stripped off his armour then rolled him into the waters of the Golden Horn. He had stared mesmerised as the dark shape, which only moments before had been his friend, bobbed down the side of the galley with arms outstretched as if in supplication as it sank below the surface. He could never forgive himself. What a coward he had been! He crouched down in the bow where he could shelter from the wind. Here in miserable isolation he picked away at his shame during the voyage home.

But the convoy sailed on, passing Troy and the Gallipoli Peninsula. The convoy put in at Imbros, Lemnos, Chios, Samos, Rhodes and Candia. At each island, refugees disembarked to return to their family homes. The fleet reduced in number until there was only one ship left going on to Venice. The winds remained favourable. No pirate ships disturbed their progress, and after two months they were drawing close to Venice. Nicolò's distress did not improve. He was no Odysseus returning in glory. He knew that when they got to Venice he would have to explain to everyone how Bartoletti had died. It weighed heavily on him.

The crew rowed past Murano, and moored in the Arsenale dockyard. There was no one to welcome him, but then no one knew he was coming home. He bade a grateful farewell to Captain Diedo. A member of the crew called over a gondola from its mooring post. Nicolò could hardly believe that he was home.

The morning sun turned the waters of the Venice lagoon to a liquid blue. The flags of Venice with their golden lions stirred in the breeze along the pavement of San Marco. The gondola slowly glided its way past the dockside of the Arsenale and the Doge's palace and into the Grand Canal up to the landing stage at the family palazzo. The seawater lifted and sank on the incoming tide making it difficult to transfer from the gondola to the pontoon, but with a helping hand from the gondolier, Nicolò stepped out of the unsteady craft. The gondolier began to mutter that he should be paid more money for his services. Then, from within the palazzo, Nicolò heard a cry of surprise. The doors opened and his mother and his father rushed out. His father flung his arms around his son.

'My boy, we thought we had lost you. We heard such terrible news, but God has brought you back to us.'

His mother wept. Her beloved son was home and that was enough for her. She wrapped her arms around him. His father looked into the gondola. 'Is Bartoletti bringing the baggage?' he asked.

'I am sorry, Father, but Bartoletti is dead. He was killed as we were leaving Constantinople.'

Nicolò could see his parents were shocked at the news, but Nicolò wanted to tell them immediately. It weighed too heavily on his conscience. Before he could speak, his father said, 'That is sad news. But we thank God that you are home. You can tell us the manner of his death later. Right now, though, your old room is ready for you. Your mother insisted that it be kept ready in case you came back unexpectedly. She was right to insist. You have come back unexpectedly. Now, it is time for lunch. We will open a bottle of chilled white wine.'

At that moment, a young servant appeared. 'Welcome back, Master Nicolò.' He bowed, seized Nicolò's hands and kissed them. His name was Joshua Aslan. He gestured towards the windows on the first floor. There, crowding the windows, were the smiling faces of the servants, men and women and young children. All dressed in workaday clothes, but the colours of their garments blended with the faded walls along the canal. Only in Venice could the servants' modest clothing look like works of art.

Nicolò had been so absorbed in his own troubles that he had forgotten what it was to be part of a family. Here he was home. He smiled back at them but a little half-heartedly, for he would have to tell them about Bartoletti and his own part in it. They welcomed him as if he were a returning hero. Nicolò feared that when they knew how he had failed Bartoletti the smiles of welcome would disappear and be replaced by the contempt that he felt for himself.

Meanwhile, the party entered the palazzo and ascended the stairs past the bales of merchandise up into the sunlit space of the reception room, which looked out over the Grand Canal. The midday sunshine poured in through the open windows with the cries of the gondoliers plying their trade, the splash of oars, the chatter of housewives and servants crossing the canal with their baskets and their children. His father and mother waived all precedence and welcomed everyone into the grand salon. As if by a miracle wine appeared, glasses were charged and toasts drunk.

Neighbours and their children entered uninvited, but on days like this no one thought of turning them away. The celebrations continued till late in the evening, and all were fed by vast platters of food washed down with Venetian wine. There was music and singing loud enough to be heard in the Piazza San Marco. All Venice joined in the celebration that one of its sons had safely returned to them.

Eventually, Nicolò was able to retreat to his own room. He spent a long time at the bedroom window looking down into the canal. How he loved this place. Then he fell exhausted onto his bed and slept deeply for the first time in many months.

He woke the next day much refreshed before remembering that he must talk to his father about Bartoletti. He could skirt around the details to avoid confessing his ignoble part in the affair. But that would not work. He would still bear the guilt without hope of forgiveness. It would be better to tell his father the truth. He dreaded this as he had never been close to his father, and their relationship in the past had been rather stiff and formal.

His father asked, 'What is it you wish to say, Nicolò?'

'Father, I must tell you about the death of Bartoletti. The truth of the matter is that I failed him when he most needed my help. I must bear responsibility for his death.'

His father's expression did not change. 'Tell me what happened, son.'

Nicolò told his father what had happened that last morning. How they had fled Constantinople after the city fell to the Turks, their brief imprisonment by the Genoese, their release and then the frantic run across the wharf to get to the ship. 'I was ahead of Bartoletti. He was carrying the instruments so was slower than I. As we neared our ship a gang of Genoese guards rushed out of the town gate. They spotted us and gave chase. Either they thought we were escaping or they wanted to take us prisoner and sell us in the slave market. I reached the ship and ran up onto the deck. The pursuers caught up with Bartoletti about ten yards from the boat. They attacked him with swords and spears like matadors goading a bull. Bartoletti turned on them, sword in hand. He kept them at bay at first, but there were eight of them. It was only a matter of time before one of them landed a blow. Bartoletti half turned, gesturing for me to come to his aid. That was the moment when I should have rushed down and charged at them. I might have saved him. But I could not move. I was afraid, you see, rooted to the deck. Then he was gone, overwhelmed. They killed him, stripped him of his armour and threw his body into the water.'

His father nodded. 'You are not a soldier, Nicolò. You were brought up to save lives not to take them. You must not be too hard on yourself. To freeze in battle is not unusual – even the bravest of men have experienced it at one time or another.'

'I must tell Mother and the staff.'

'Leave that to me. I will tell everyone who needs to know. The truth is that Bartoletti died bravely fighting to protect you, the son of our family. The man was a soldier and a loyal servant. I promised him his freedom if he brought you safely home. He kept his promise to bring you home and I will keep my promise to him to grant his freedom. It will be our family's gesture of gratitude to a good man. As to the matter of your feeling responsible for his death, that is between yourself and your conscience. If you must confess, go to the priests in church – they will grant you absolution. Pay the priests to say a Mass for Bartoletti. But don't go around telling everyone in Venice that you were a coward. First of all, you are not a coward, and secondly, it would damage

146

our family's standing if you insist on playing the penitent. You need to put this behind you. You are a doctor. Be one here in Venice. You could be a good doctor, perhaps a great one. I think we need more physicians and fewer soldiers in this world.'

Nicolò was surprised at how wise his father had become. They had never talked about such matters in the past. His father had been preoccupied with business and affairs of state. Now they were talking man to man, openly and honestly.

'I will take your advice, Father. Thank you.'

'You will need to meet with the Doge and his council. Tell them what happened in Constantinople as a result of their failure to send help. Sometimes politicians need to be reminded that decisions taken around a table far away from the action can result in unimaginable suffering.'

14

Reporting to Council
August 1453

 o sooner had Nicolò's father left the room than his mother entered. She was full of joy at his unexpected return but knew nothing of the conversation with his father. She said, 'Nicolò, I want you to tell me all about your travels.'

Nicolò, in jest, replied, 'Just to reassure you, before you ask, Mother, I am not married. The young ladies in Constantinople were very beautiful, but I managed to avoid committing to any marriage contracts. Like here, mothers in Constantinople seemed to think that a Venetian surgeon would be a good catch.'

His mother knew that he was teasing her. She noticed however that he did not rule out the possibility of marriage in the future. Perhaps she should start to draw up a new list of candidates. But, patience; it was too soon to rush things. She studied her son. He was looking out of the window but thinking of other things. She saw how thin his face had become. His cheekbones were more prominent and he was worn out and grey and exhausted. It seemed to his mother that some inner light had been extinguished. She wondered what had happened to him in Constantinople to have this effect.

She said gently, 'Nicolò, you are home, that's what counts. Promise that you will not leave us again.'

He looked at his mother. She was an elegant woman impeccably dressed as a Venetian lady of high standing. He noticed that the silk morning dress she was wearing showed off her well-rounded form to advantage. The jewels about her wrists were large and ostentatious and she was wrapped in the musky scent of an expensive perfume.

Before leaving on his travels Nicolò had been contemptuous of the wealth and display of his parents and their palazzo on the Grand Canal. But perhaps he had been too hasty. After the traumas of Constantinople, he put a higher value on their support, and found it reassuring to have a place to call home. Here in Venice he could knock on his parents' door and it would always be opened to him. In fact, that was true of many doors in Venice where he had friends and family. Constantinople had been exotic, but it had proved to be a chimera, an illusion and a fantasy of youth. The memories of his time there left a bitter taste.

The next week, he talked again to his father. 'I should like to meet with the Doge to give him my report on what happened in Constantinople, and I want his advice on what I should do next.'

His father nodded. 'I will arrange for you to meet him later this week.'

So, on the following Friday, Nicolò entered the Doge's study for the second time. It was the same room as two years earlier. The Doge looked even more world-weary if that were possible. He looked up from the papers on his desk, and said, 'Young man, first I should like to thank you for your reports which I know were sent at some considerable risk to yourself. You pleaded the cause of Constantinople most eloquently. In fact there were times when I felt you had become a little too emotionally attached to the Byzantine cause. If you continue to work for me you might need to learn a little more detachment.'

Nicolò noted both the implied criticism but also the hint that he might continue to work for the Doge. He was no longer afraid to make his views known. 'I am a doctor not a diplomat. In my reports I put down what I felt at the time. The warnings I gave of the Byzantine situation proved to be accurate. The city has fallen. With more support from Venice that need not have happened. Another five thousand fighting men would have been sufficient to repel the Turks. Why did you not send the fleet to save the city?'

The Doge hesitated. 'The Council of Ten debated sending reinforcements on many occasions but they were split on what action to take. In the end they did nothing and our fleet remained in port. In my view that was the right decision. Council had to balance the trading interests of Venice against the cost of propping up an ailing Byzantine regime, and, of course, sending aid to Constantinople would have involved us in war with the Turks.'

The Doge took Nicolò by the arm and guided him to the mullioned window. 'Look down there, my boy. See the warehouses, the markets, the trading galleys and the shipyards. All these depend on our ability to trade around the world, not just the Christian world but the countries of the Middle East and Far East. Business and trade flourish in time of peace. Venice becomes richer. War impoverishes everyone. I realise that for an idealistic young man putting profit before saving the Byzantine Empire might seem poor-spirited.'

Nicolò was annoyed by the Doge's patronising tone. He had no doubt now that the selfish interests of Venetian merchants had been behind the failure to send help. The decisions of Council had been a piece of cynical self-interest. Their decisions were justified, no doubt, by lengthy debates in Council but stripped down were about money and profit. It was an example of power politics rather than of doing the right thing. He was sick at heart when he recalled the dead and dying on the battlements of Constantinople. No one here cared that lives had been lost by brave men in an attempt to preserve the Byzantine Empire.

He could not resist saying, 'There are many good men and women who lie dead in the streets of Constantinople as a result of your nice calculations, Your Excellency.' Realising he had overstepped the mark, he said, 'I apologise, Your Excellency. I have spoken out too boldly.'

The Doge turned his tired eyes towards Nicolò. 'Young man, thank God someone still speaks the truth. In my world no one speaks the truth and they shape what they say by self-interest.'

The Doge was not telling the whole truth about his attitude towards helping the Byzantines. Before Constantine became Emperor, the Doge had proposed that Constantine should marry his own daughter, promising to provide her with a handsome dowry. Constantine had agreed to the Doge's proposal, but the marriage did not go ahead because a Doge's daughter was not considered to be of high enough rank to become the wife of a Byzantine Emperor. It seemed that the Doge had not sent reinforcements to Constantinople, in part, because he felt his family had been slighted by Constantine.

The Doge continued, 'Now what are we going to do with you? You are too outspoken to be a diplomat, unsuited to being a soldier and have no interest in commerce. What you do have is experience of battlefield medicine and saving the lives of wounded soldiers. I understand that you organised medical facilities within the Byzantine armed forces and the civilian population during the siege. Could you do something similar here?'

Nicolò was surprised by this suggestion. He had expected to set up a private medical practice in Venice or Padua. What the Doge had in mind was a much more important role. Even so, he did not rush to accept the Doge's offer. He had learnt from past dealings with the Doge that you should not seem too eager.

'May I think about your suggestion and come back to you within the month?'

'Of course, young man. Take your time. I understand your reluctance, given the circumstances. You might like to attend the Council of Ten next week to present your report. Council will also hear from another eye witness, a certain sea captain, who will report on what happened after the Turks took the city. I understand that you had left by then so it will interest you as well no doubt.'

'I should like to attend,' Nicolò replied.

Therefore, the following week, he attended the meeting in the Venetian Council Chamber. It was a very grand room with its sweeping ceiling and, on the walls, portraits, flags and statues proclaiming the importance and prestige of the Venetian State. It was meant to impress overseas dignitaries. The Doge sat on a gilded seat at the head of the table where each of the ten council members had their designated place. It was customary to stand when addressing Council.

Nicolò was there to report on his work as medical officer in Constantinople. He kept his speech short. The Doge had circulated copies of his reports to which he drew their attention. He spoke only of the events of the last days before the Turkish assault, the assault itself and the fall of the city. He told them that the Emperor had sent a ship to look for the Venetian fleet in the Aegean and of his despair when no fleet could be found. Even at the end the Emperor had posted lookouts in hope of sighting the Venetian fleet bringing reinforcements. The Emperor had trusted in the promises of the Venetians.

After he finished speaking, the Doge asked if there were any questions. There were none. Members did not want to get into a debate as to why the Venetian fleet had not reached Constantinople. The room fell silent. Was their silence an admission of guilt? More likely the fall of Constantinople was, in their minds, a fait accompli and further discussion was pointless. Nicolò had intended to spell out in graphic terms the effects of their inaction, but his nerve failed him faced with a wall of impassive and self-satisfied faces. He referred them to his diary record which was to be lodged in the Venetian archives should they wish for a fuller account of the siege.

The Doge then introduced Zuane Loredan, a Venetian sea

captain recently arrived from Constantinople. The captain was invited to give his account of the events. Captain Loredan, a well-built man with grizzled hair and sunburned face, explained that he and his crew had manned a section of the city wall near the Emperor's palace.

He reported as follows: 'I was present when the Emperor Constantine gave his instructions to his court officials, the tribunes, the centurions and other noble soldiers before the final assault. The Emperor said, and I abbreviate his words, "You are all experienced and seasoned warriors – courageous, well prepared. I advise you to protect your heads with your shields. Keep your right hand, with the sword, extended in front of you at all times. Your helmets, breastplates and suits of armour are fully sufficient together with your other weapons and will prove very effective in combat. You are protected by the city walls, while they, in contrast, will advance without cover and with toil. Let us force our enemy to depart from here in shame."'

Captain Loredan described how the Emperor mounted his horse and toured the land walls with George Sphrantzes by his side. They checked that the sentinels were alert, telling them to report the movements of the enemy and to make sure that all the doors into the towers were securely locked. Then the Emperor ascended the tower at the Kaligaria Gate to ascertain the intentions of the Turks. 'We heard much shouting and noise from the enemy,' Captain Loredan continued. 'Then, without any warning, three hours before daybreak, the Turks attacked. As the sky lightened, I could see that the enemy had surrounded the whole periphery of the city like the rope around the neck of a condemned man. The defenders hurled down rocks, liquid fire, catapult missiles and arrows. They fired artillery pieces into the crowds of the enemy killing many. The Christians taunted the Turks – "Even though you have tried so many times, you have failed miserably." But in places I noticed that the walls were beginning to collapse under the relentless Turkish fire. The enemy concentrated their attacks at those points where the damage to the walls was greatest. Mighty battles ensued of hand-to-hand fighting with naked swords. Many were killed on both sides. The Christian defenders held the line thanks to the bravery of men such as Theophilos Palaeologus and Demetrios Kantakouzenos, who pushed the enemy ladders away from the walls. The Emperor continued to encourage his men. He said, "Stand your ground firmly, my brothers and fellow soldiers. I detect that the multitude of the enemy is beginning to break up. They are being scattered. I hope to God that victory is ours. God is on our side and cowardice is invading the multitude of the impious."

Loredan continued, 'It was at this moment that an arrow pierced Giovanni Giustiniani, commander of the land forces, in his right leg just above the foot. His former bravery evaporated when he saw blood spurting from his wound. He left his post without a word to get medical help. When his soldiers turned and could not see their general, they lost their spirit and cohesion. Hasan, the Janissary, led an attack with thirty others, routing our defenders and driving them back from the walls. They shouted, "The castle has fallen. Turkish standards and banners have been raised on the towers."

'Constantine saw what was happening. He spurred on his horse and reached the spot where the Turks were coming over the walls in greatest numbers. He fought like Samson against the Philistines. Roaring like a lion and holding his sword in his right hand, he killed many, while blood was streaming from his legs and arms. At his side were Don Francisco from Toledo, Theophiles Palaeologus and John Dalmates, who displayed great bravery. They and a group of other noble knights put many of the impious to flight and inflicted heavy damage. But finally they were overwhelmed by the weight of opposing numbers and died with great courage.

'The Turks swept into the city like a tidal wave which heaves itself up from the ocean floor. Those on the beach could see the wave coming from far off but as fast as they ran, it caught and drowned them. At this point, I and my platoon abandoned our position on the city wall. It was no longer possible to hold when other Christian forces were retreating. The streets were littered with dead men, women and children. All the buildings had been broken into and the doors stood agape. Turkish flags flew from the roofs of houses to show they had been searched. We passed a hospital near the Romanus Gate. Inside were lines of wounded soldiers lying as if asleep on stretchers, but on inspection all their throats had been cut. The nuns, who knew only lives of prayer, had been raped then chained together to be sent to the slave market. Some terrified women threw themselves to their deaths from the walls or into wells. The enemy were lusting for blood and desire to avenge their fallen comrades. The cobbled streets ran with blood. We hurried down to the harbour where we boarded our ship.'

Captain Loredan finished speaking. The Council Chamber was deathly quiet. The Doge asked for questions. There were no questions. The Doge thanked the captain for his honest account which had moved them all.

As the captain was making his way out of the chamber, Nicolò took him aside. 'Captain Loredan, I am Barbaro, doctor of the field hospital near the Romanus Gate. I had to leave before the Turks arrived. Was there any way I could have saved those men and women?'

The captain looked him straight in the eye. 'Your staying would have made no difference, but in my opinion you should not have left your patients to die in the way that they did.'

15

Lunch with George Sphrantzes
August 1454

icolò accepted the Doge's offer to become Superintendent of Medical Services a month after the meeting. The month gave him the chance to plan how he would undertake such an onerous task. He wanted to start his own medical practice alongside the work for the armed services so did not want to commit more than half his time to working for the Doge. It was no easy task to prepare a plan, given Venice's numerous interests in the Mediterranean and Aegean. The potential need for military medical services differed, dependant on the scale of their naval and land forces in the area and the threat from enemies.

He started by plotting on a map all the places where Venice had military establishments, including castles, camps, ports and naval ships. Against each place he noted the present number and type of naval and military forces and any changes foreseen. He estimated likely threats by talking to military leaders. There could be no absolutely right and wrong answers, but hopefully the exercise would give them an idea of possible casualty figures in the event of war and allow him to decide on any increase needed in facilities and medical supplies. It was a big task. He put together a team of advisors from the armed services to help him to frame a strategy to make specific recommendations. Nicolò visited some locations himself – at least those near Venice. For more distant places, he sent out surveys which had to be completed by local commanders and returned to his office in the Doge's Palace.

His recommendations were well received by the religious communities since he proposed to pay them an annual fee for providing a reserve of beds, operating theatres, stocks of medicines and other supplies. Nicolò prepared training courses, operating manuals and a primer for surgery on war wounds based on his experience in Constantinople. Researchers at Padua University contributed to the development of these initiatives, and helped to organise and run training courses for staff and volunteers. He presented his proposals to the Doge and the Council of Ten in June 1454. Council agreed his plan, and allotted the funding for an initial five hundred-bed reserve with capacity to expand the number up to two thousand beds in time of war.

Nicolò became totally immersed in this task. The work helped to speed his recovery after the traumatic events he had witnessed in Constantinople. His parents were delighted that Nicolò had rediscovered his enthusiasm for medicine. The haggard look had been replaced by a filling out of his features and a healthier complexion. His smile had returned. He began to visit his old friends from Padua, no longer spending days alone in his room. That worrying phase had passed. He visited friends' homes and dined with them in the evenings, becoming a favourite uncle to their children.

He spoke to friends about the fall of Constantinople if they asked. Naturally, he said nothing about Bartoletti and how he had died. Some of his friends wanted to dramatise the whole thing and make him into a hero, and he did his best to deflect such misplaced admiration. He encouraged friends to read and critique his diary which recorded the events leading to the fall of Constantinople. As the weeks passed, he convinced himself that his failures had resulted from being under extreme pressure, the like of which he might never encounter again in his lifetime – this proved to be an over-optimistic assumption. It was as if all his failings had somehow been the responsibility of someone else. He resolved to stop looking at the past. Instead he would concentrate on building a future in Venice.

As a part of the process of recovery, he decided that he must make confession as his father had suggested. With this in mind, he went to a local church one weekday at an hour when he knew that he was unlikely to meet anyone he knew. In a side chapel, he noticed a priest sitting by the confessional reading his breviary while waiting for penitents to come into the church. Nicolò entered the confessional and knelt down by the grille which the priest slid open when he heard him enter. Nicolò spoke the words he had learned as a schoolboy: 'Father, forgive me for I have sinned.' He confessed to the priest the matters troubling his conscience in the same words he had used to his father. He held nothing back. He remembered the words of the prophet Isaiah: 'For our faults in your sight have been many and our sins are a witness against us and indeed our faults are present to our minds, and we know our iniquities.'

The priest listened attentively, and said, 'My son, you have a heavy burden to bear, but God understands human weakness and you have made a sincere confession. For your penance say ten Our Fathers and offer a Mass for those you failed.' The priest then pronounced the words of absolution, ending with, 'Go in peace. Your sins are forgiven you.' With those words, a great load was lifted. Now, he was confident that God had absolved him from his guilt. The priest closed the grille. Nicolò stood up and walked back into the chapel. He knelt for a few minutes to say his penance. He arranged with the priest for a Mass to be offered the following week. He left the church and went into the sun-filled street renewed in spirit.

It was a shock when, shortly after this, he received a message from George Sphrantzes. It was the first he had heard of him since leaving Constantinople. George explained in his note that he was on his way to Rome on a diplomatic mission for the Emperor's brother, Thomas. He suggested that they meet while he was in Venice. Nicolò did not entirely welcome this intrusion from his old friend. Inevitably they would talk about Constantinople which would bring back painful memories. But there was nothing for it but to invite George for lunch. On seeing him, Nicolò was taken aback. He was a shadow of the man whom he had known in Constantinople. It was as if his friend had suffered some serious illness or other tragedy. Gone was the arrogant historian, the friend and confidant of emperors and kings. This man looked more like an impoverished cleric.

They sat at a table overlooking the Grand Canal and ate a simple lunch of bread, cheese and olives, and drank a glass of local wine. Nicolò was briefly distracted as he watched the sunshine refracting through the glass of white wine throwing patterns of green and yellow onto the table. Then George said, 'I heard that you had left Constantinople. I was relieved to hear you managed to escape.'

'Yes, I was fortunate, but I was very concerned for you and your family.'

'There was nothing you could have done for us. Bartoletti took us to the monastery and the monks hid us for three days at great danger to themselves. We were probably saved by the Sultan's order that all the buildings and their treasures belonged to him. The Turkish soldiers battered on the door but did not try to force entry.'

'How are your wife and children? Were they sold as slaves when you surrendered to the Turks?'

'They were fortunate at first in becoming the property of an elderly Turkish couple who lived in Adrianople. They were treated with kindness and in return Helene helped with the education of their children. Unfortunately, they were then sold on to the Sultan's Master of Horse who was looking to make a profit on his investment and regularly traded in captives. A household servant informed him there were two beautiful children in the house. The Sultan's procurer, the Black Aga, was told about the children, raided the house and bore them off to the seraglio. Do you remember how delightful our children were? Well, this monstrous creature purchased them for the Sultan. Helene was left alone with only the nurse to comfort her. She endured slavery for a year before I could raise the money for her ransom.

'But, Nicolò, I have to tell you that my son, John, is dead. He was killed in the seraglio. He must have known that it was only a matter of time before the Sultan would ask for him. They tell me he hid a dagger in his clothing, intending to kill Mehmed rather than submit to him. However, the Sultan was well protected and the eunuchs discovered the knife. The Sultan took the life of my dearest son with his own hand. The lad was only fourteen years old. He killed my dear son, that most impious and pitiless of men.

George continued bitterly, 'I arrived in Adrianople too late to save them. Do you recall how happy the children were when we had lunch together in the garden? The plans they made? Tamar was going to be a friend to the Emperor's bride when she arrived in Constantinople. John was coming with me to Georgia. They were so happy and excited and looking forward to their lives. Now John is dead and Tamar is imprisoned in the seraglio. Thank God we cannot see the future. Do you remember them?'

Nicolò replied, 'Of course I remember them, George. I hope Mehmed rots in hell for what he did!'

George answered, 'And yet I forgive him. Can you hold a wild beast responsible for killing its prey? My children were vulnerable prey and I was not there to protect them. My human nature tells me to hate the man. As a Christian, I must forgive him.'

Nicolò wondered how George could forgive the man who had murdered his son and imprisoned his daughter. Surely that was asking too much even of a Christian.

George said that his wife Helene had been distraught since the loss of her son. It had proved too much for her fragile mind. She had given birth to five children, and now four of her children were dead, and she could never forgive him for insisting that they stay in Constantinople when they could have escaped to Chios.

She, an emperor's niece, had endured slavery for over a year until he ransomed her one year later. It was the final blow. Helene left him, choosing the seclusion of a convent in Corfu over married life. After a year, she took her final vows and joined the order. George was told by the sisters that she was unwell and in frail health.

The two friends finished their lunch in sober mood. George was sailing for Rome later in the day on a diplomatic mission for the Emperor's brother. They parted amicably. Nicolò felt for his friend's sadness. How frail and elderly George had become! He had lost so much – children, wife, wealth, country and his emperor. Yes, he had lost all the things that had once been his joy, his reason for living.

'Is there anything I can do to help, George? Do you need funds? You are welcome to stay with my family,' Nicolò offered.

'Thank you, my friend, but I will manage. By the way, did you complete your diary?'

Nicolò smiled. 'You have an excellent memory, George. It is complete except for final editing. You are, of course, a key player in the drama. It was a drama, wasn't it? Like one of those Greek tragedies in which men are destroyed by their own pride and at the whim of the gods.'

George seemed rather put out by the description of his life as part of a Greek tragedy. In George's mind, the comparison diminished the importance of his experience of real life. His family had experienced enough sadness without needing to write a play about it.

The ship for Rome sailed that evening with George on board.

16

I Nozze di Nicolò

(Nicolò Gets Married)

September 1455

ou eat alone was not a compliment in Venice. A man who eats alone is, by inference, a bachelor and therefore not contributing fully to family life in Venetian society. So when his mother said to Nicolò, 'You eat alone at the table', he knew his bachelor days were numbered. He was happy being a bachelor, and enjoyed spending evenings with his unmarried friends, drinking a cool glass of wine and admiring the mothers and daughters, arm in arm, as they strolled around the Piazza San Marco. He had noticed, however, that the number of his unattached friends was gradually reducing.

Equally ominous were his mother's next words: "I have been discussing things with your father and we are agreed that you are quite old enough to get married – you are almost thirty. Your father has asked me to find you a suitable wife. Your sisters married well, but their dowries cost your father a great deal, more than we could really afford. Your father hopes to offset some of that cost with your bride's dowry.' It was beginning to sound a little too mercenary so his mother changed tack. 'You can see how happy your friends are now they are married and how much you enjoy being a favourite uncle. You will make a wonderful husband and father.'

Nicolò reluctantly admitted, 'I suppose I shall have to marry one day.'

His mother detected a crumbling of resistance. 'Yes, Nicolò, and the sooner the better, I think. You need a dowry to finance the start-up of your practice.'

'But,' Nicolò responded, 'it is all a bit theoretical. I don't know anyone I would want to marry even for their dowry. My friends have already married the best women in Venice. How do I go about finding someone?'

His mother knew she had won. 'Now, Nicolò, I will find a wife for you, but you must promise me that you will not change your mind. It was so embarrassing last time when you upset my friends and their daughters by running away to Constantinople.'

Nicolò promised his mother that he would do his best not to let her down. He did not think that he had run away last time. No, he had needed to explore the world before he settled down.

'Nicolò, I will do my best. Hopefully, I can find somebody to take you off my hands!'

Nicolò had not considered the possibility of being turned down, such is the vanity of young men.

His mother explained the sort of young woman she would be looking for.

'She must be from a patrician family, aged between eighteen and twenty-two, well-educated, and able to speak and read Greek, Latin and, of course, Italian. She must be at ease in society and accomplished in the arts and music and her reputation must be unblemished without any hint of impropriety. I will talk to my friends and engage the services of a matchmaker to widen the choice. The widow Contessa Francessi is the most talented matchmaker in Venice. I have spoken to her and she is prepared to act for us. If anyone can find you a bride, she can. I will arrange for her to visit us tomorrow morning.'

The following day, the Contessa Francessi arrived. She was an imposing woman of middle years, above average height and of ample girth. Her hair was an auburn mass of untended curls, her eyes a piercing blue. Expensive clothes hung luxuriously from her shoulders, and she wore a necklace studded with amethysts around her neck. Her fingers were heavy with ostentatious rings. In a forceful and commanding voice she addressed him:

'Nicolò, your mother has asked me to find you a wife. Please assure me that you really want to get married. Are you determined? You will need to be for faint heart never won fair lady.'

Nicolò tried to sound suitably resolute. 'Contessa, I am determined to marry if you can find me the right wife.'

'Why do you think any young woman would want to marry you?'

Nicolò was wrong-footed by the forceful Contessa's challenging tone. He tried to think of reasons why someone might want to marry him. 'Well, my family is wealthy and well regarded in Venetian society. My father's business is successful and will grow even larger if we are allied to another prosperous family. My mother tells me that I am not bad-looking and can even be charming if necessary. Overall, I think most young women would consider me a good catch.'

The Contessa replied, 'You are conceited like most Venetian men, sadly. Still, I have learned to work with such unsatisfactory material. Now, what sort of wife do you want? I assume you have given that some thought. In my experience most Venetian women are beautiful but vain, self-absorbed and only interested in clothes, dances and entertainment. They want a successful husband who will provide them with houses, jewels and clothes. Then there is a much smaller number of women who crave education, self-improvement and a role in society. These are clever women who will challenge a man. They make excellent wives if their husbands are not afraid of wives with independent minds and can accept a wife as his equal.'

Nicolò was taken aback. It was more complicated than he had expected. His friends had happily settled for wives in the first group – pretty women, laden with jewels and comfortable in society. Their husbands showed them off as if they were sporting trophies.

'Well, put like that, without having given it much thought, I would say that an educated young woman is more likely to suit me. I am sure I will know the right woman if and when I meet her.'

The Contessa put no trust in instinctual reaction. 'Your mother and I have agreed that a young woman of intelligence would suit you best. You are a bookish sort of man and a scientist. Most women don't want such men as husbands – they tend to be boring.'

Nicolò had not thought of himself as being bookish. Was he really so boring? Was that how he appeared to the outside world?

The Contessa continued, 'Before this meeting, I took the liberty of making a list of educated young women whom I would be happy to recommend. It is a short list, a very short list. Venice is not blessed with many educated women seeking to improve their minds. I have only three names. Your mother and I will arrange for you to view each of these girls at Sunday Mass – one a week. She will not know she is being observed by a prospective husband. If you like one of them enough, I can arrange an introduction.'

Nicolò readily agreed. He would be intrigued to see the three young women as soon as possible. After all, why not look?

The Contessa continued, 'Their names are Francesca Foscarini, Isabella Carpaccio and Clara Foscari. You will attend the midday Mass at San Marco on the next three Sundays. These young women will be there with their families.'

Sunday Mass in San Marco was a social as well as a religious event. On Sunday morning the cathedral was full of worshippers. Fathers gathered in the corners of the cathedral to discuss business, leaving their families to look after themselves. The Mass carried on in the background without anyone taking much notice. The interior was dark, lit by candlelight. Every inch of the walls and interior was covered in gold mosaics; it was a very beautiful and comforting place.

Nicolò leaned against a pillar in the portico as the congregation began to leave at the end of Mass. Mostly it was family groups. As they escaped, there were cheerful sounds of friends greeting each other, young girls laughing in their conspiratorial way, and boys shouting as they ran away across the piazza, free at last.

Francesca Foscarini, the first on the Contessa's list, walked out of Mass with her father and mother. He recognised her from the Contessa's description. She was quite tall with blonde hair pulled back off her face. Her hair was held in place by a silk band of silver cloth. She wore a becoming gown of the same colour, and had a pearl necklace around her long thin neck. Her face was pale and her nose was pointed. She looked a most determined and clever young woman. Nicolò decided there and then that she would not make a comfortable wife.

The following Sunday, he returned to the same spot. This time it was to view Isabella Carpaccio, daughter of a rich merchant. Her family group strolled confidently into the piazza. They were in no hurry and made a leisurely circuit with friends and admirers. Isabella Carpaccio was hauntingly beautiful. Her golden hair fell in ringlets onto her bosom which was modestly but lightly shrouded in the blue silk of her dress. Her face had that symmetry so admired by artists. She was the essence of feminine beauty. But, was she too perfect, too beautiful? Nicolò decided that he was uncomfortable with such perfection. Could he trust her to remain faithful to a dull, bookish man like himself? Would he have to spend his life fending off her admirers?

On the next Sunday Nicolò thought he might have missed Clara Foscari among the crowds which streamed out of the great doors of San Marco, but then he recognised her brother who had also been at medical school in Padua. The girl next to him must be Clara Foscari. She was not a beauty like Isabella Carpaccio, but she was attractive and blessed with the natural bloom which is the gift of nature to the young. Her face was pleasingly symmetrical and delicately formed. She wore a thin gold chain around her head from which an amethyst rested on the centre of her forehead. Her woollen dress was rose, interwoven with silk thread, and she wore a necklace of gold and precious stones. At that moment, just as he was observing her, she turned to talk to her mother. In turning, she looked directly at Nicolò leaning against a pillar. Perhaps she recognised him as her brother's friend. She gave him a warm and spontaneous smile of recognition. He returned her smile. She continued to walk out of the cathedral, but just as she passed through the great doors, she looked back over her shoulder. It was the briefest of glances but he had no doubt that this time she was looking at him.

He told his mother, 'I want to marry Clara Foscari!'

His mother was pleased with his choice which agreed with her own decision. Clara Foscari was the Doge's niece and socially more than acceptable. 'I think she would do very well, Nicolò.'

The Contessa outlined the process now that he had made his choice. She warned Nicolò that it would take some weeks, even if the families agreed to the match, so he must be patient. Nicolò, of course, had made up his mind and wanted her as his wife straightaway. But, as the Contessa made clear, there were many steps before he could expect to marry her.

'The two families must meet informally to agree that the marriage is in the interests of both families. At this meeting the prospective bride and groom will be introduced. After the introduction they will be permitted a brief, more personal meeting in the presence of a chaperone. If the bride and groom are in agreement, the formal procedures will go ahead with the preparation and signing of the contract of engagement. The contract includes the amount and composition of the bride's dowry. After the exchange of contracts, the engagement is publicly announced in the presence of both families and state officials. The next stage is the showing forth of the bride around family houses and the public declaration of their matrimonial vows. Sponsors, usually trade associates, make gifts to the bride and groom – in this case the guild of medical professionals. Other rituals will include the exchange of rings and visits by the bride to convents where she has relatives. The showing of the bride symbolises the bride's commitment to produce the next generation of the family. Then there will be a number of feasts before the wedding. The marriage ceremony will be conducted by a cardinal in San Marco. The final act is for the bride to be led to the bridegroom's house. The marriage can then be consummated.' The Contessa assured him that the families, officials, and she herself, would see to everything.

But the first step must be for the prospective bride and groom to meet one another to confirm that they wanted to go ahead. The introduction was to take place the following weekend.

That Saturday morning Nicolò woke in a state of excitement. Today he would meet his future wife. He hoped that his first impressions had been right, but he was afraid that he might be disappointed when he met her. He was also worried that she might be disappointed with the bookish doctor and dusty scientist the Contessa had described. He had no idea of the sort of husband Clara wanted. He had the vague impression that young women spent days in romantic speculation about their future husbands. He dreaded the thought that when they were introduced, her face would betray her disappointment with him.

Nicolò, his parents and the Contessa arrived by gondola at the bride's family palazzo on the Grand Canal. They were led up a flight of stone steps to a reception room on the first floor. Here a rather grand servant dressed in livery instructed them to wait. Clara's father and mother entered a few minutes later. They offered light refreshments to their guests. Her father cast a cold eye over his prospective son-in-law. Nicolò was in no doubt that without the endorsement of the Doge, her father would much prefer a man of business for his daughter. There was not much money in curing the sick. However, the Doge had reassured him that the young man was capable in his own field and that he had acted with bravery during the siege of Constantinople. Her father had relayed this endorsement to his wife and daughter.

Unfortunately, the Contessa told Nicolò that his courageous actions in Constantinople had helped to secure the father's agreement. For Nicolò, this was the worst possible news. How could he marry Clara Foscari without telling her about his ignominious role in the death of Bartoletti? He could not let her think that he was a hero when he was no such thing. He must tell her. At that moment, an interior door opened and Clara came into the salon. She was dressed in her finest gown as befitted the occasion. He smiled and she returned his smile. He offered his hand and she took it. Her hand was trembling a little. She was nervous.

She said quietly, 'Dottore, our families intend us to marry. I am willing to marry you.'

He replied with the same formality, 'It is my greatest hope that you will become my wife.'

The formal words had been spoken. So everyone was surprised when Nicolò asked Clara's parents, 'May I talk to your daughter in private for a moment?'

Her parents consulted the Contessa, who confirmed that there was precedent for such a personal discussion provided a chaperone was present. The Contessa was not happy with his request. What was he going to say? The young doctor was sorely trying her patience.

The couple withdraw to an alcove by the window, accompanied by a chaperone. They stood by the window watching the Grand Canal bustling with Venetian life. The noises from the canal, the shouts of the boatmen, and the banging of gondolas against their mooring posts in the tide swell, penetrated into the room.

Nicolò, in a nervous rush, told Clara of his flight from Constantinople, the desertion of his patients and the death of Bartoletti. 'You see, Clara, I am no hero as your father seems to think. In fact, I behaved despicably in not saving my friend. I could not get married without telling you the truth.'

Clara was shocked by this confession. It was so unexpected. Did he want to marry her or was this his way of putting her off? What other things might he be hiding from her? It was outside her experience. She could think of nothing to say. The truth blocked the way to their engagement as surely as an avalanche blocks a mountain pass.

The Contessa saw that things had taken a turn for the worse. Without hesitating, she crossed the room and went straight up to the couple. 'My dears, can I help?'

Clara told the Contessa what Nicolò had told her. Tearfully, she said, 'I suppose it is all off now.'

The Contessa was never lost for words even in the most trying of circumstances. Really, this young man was proving very difficult. Her arrangement fee was slipping from her grasp. This man was suffering from an over-active conscience. Surely he had reached the age when he must realise that speaking the truth was sometimes positively harmful.

She took them further into the alcove. 'Clara, do you want to marry the dottore? Dottore, do you wish to marry this lovely young woman?' They both nodded and the Contessa continued, 'I must tell you that in my experience everyone who gets married has a guilty conscience about something or other. Nicolò, you are very wrong to burden your prospective bride with such matters at this late stage. Bartoletti is gone. Let him rest in peace. He would not want his death to prevent your marriage. He gave his life for you. It will all work out. I cannot remember a couple so well suited. I am quite sure you will find happiness if you marry.'

The Contessa's firm words did the trick. They looked at each other with fresh eyes. Clara saw an unhappy man much in need of kindness, love and forgiveness. She could give him these things. She wanted to be his wife. Nicolò saw a loving companion to whom he could talk without inhibition. He had already told her the worst. They knew the Contessa was right and that they were well suited. They agreed to go ahead without more ado. They moved back into the centre of the room, their faces mirroring their inner happiness. The families embraced the couple warmly. The formal contract of marriage could now be drawn up and signed.

That evening, Clara's father said to his wife, 'That Contessa is worth every penny of her fee. I thought it was all going wrong when they looked so miserable. The Contessa found the key whatever it was.'

Clara's mother replied, 'Yes, I think they will do well together. Let's get them married quickly before that young doctor has any more second thoughts.'

Her husband concurred, and just two weeks later the marriage contract was signed. In the contract, the amount of the bride's dowry was set out as a matter of public record. The total value was five thousand ducats – generous but not ruinous. The bride's father was pleased that he could afford it without unduly denting the profits of his business.

The way was clear to fix a date. Two months was the minimum time needed to complete the formalities. A week must be set aside for feasting before the wedding itself, with up to three hundred guests expected to attend formal dinners. Because Clara was a relative of the Doge, a number of foreign ambassadors were invited. It would be an important social event. The two months passed quickly. The final week of indulgence in food and wine Nicolò found exhausting. He just wanted to get it all over and marry this girl.

The Contessa took Clara aside one morning. It was part of her duties to make sure that her girls, as she called them, were instructed in the facts of life before the wedding. It never ceased to amaze her how ignorant brides were as to what would be required of them on their wedding night. Mothers tended to duck the issue, but the Contessa had no such inhibitions. She explained it all in great detail. She jested that God must have had a sense of humour when he devised the strange manoeuvres needed for procreation. 'You might learn to like it,' she told Clara. 'Don't treat it as a duty to be endured but as a pleasure to be enjoyed.'

The wedding day arrived. The wedding service itself was held in San Marco. There were over three hundred guests, including a number of notables who attended because the bride was related to the Doge. The wedding was incorporated into High Mass celebrated by the cardinal, assistant priests, altar boys and the many religious known to the two families. The cathedral choir sang splendidly. The couple exchanged vows and rings.

The couple were now married, but the important celebrations were still to follow. The bride and groom and their guests walked across the piazza and boarded the Doge's magnificent skiff, *Il Buccantorre*, which was moored at the San Marco pavement. From late afternoon until late in the night there were musical performances, plays, mimes and dancing as the elegant galley was rowed up and down the Grand Canal. When the ship passed under the Rialto Bridge it turned back and returned to San Marco. It continued on this circuit to the delight of the guests and the citizens of Venice leaning precariously over the bridge to enjoy the spectacle. The children complained bitterly when they had to leave. Everyone agreed that it had been an occasion worthy even of Venice.

Eventually, the guests began to take their leave. They were still full of song and dancing and in the best of spirits. The bride and groom, with their families, were the last to disembark at San Marco. There Clara said a tearful farewell to her mother and father who had cared for her throughout her life. Now she must leave them to enter the home of strangers. Nicolò, his sisters and family escorted her to her new home which was near enough for Clara to see her parents' home if she leaned out of the window.

When they arrived at Nicolò's family palazzo only the consummation of the marriage remained. Other members of the family retired discreetly to their rooms. Clara was escorted by her sisters-in-law and the chambermaids to the marital bedchamber. The maids had dressed the room with sweet-smelling candles, spices and herbs and had hung tapestries around the bed decorated with scenes from antiquity of an amorous nature. The maids helped Clara to undress. They eased the delicate nightdress made of finest golden silk over her head, then laughingly helped Clara clamber up into the marital bed to await her husband. She admitted to her maid that she was apprehensive.

'Don't you worry, signora. He's a lovely man. He could have had any woman in Venice. He chose you.'

Clara composed herself for the arrival of her husband. She did not have to wait long. He came into the room a little hesitantly as if he were an intruder entering the forbidden temple of a Vestal Virgin. Seeing her waiting for him, he was captivated by her beauty and grace. He hesitantly crossed the room and took her hand, kissing it gently. At that moment, he felt a passion to possess her but was anxious not to alarm her. Then he kissed her lightly on the lips. Her response was surprisingly eager. Encouraged, he drew her into his arms and sank down beside her. That night, they took a mutual delight in each other, fulfilling their natural desires and experienced the intense joy of belonging completely to one other.

Early the next day, as the sun rose up from the languid lagoon, the new husband and wife took breakfast together for the first time on the balcony overlooking the Grand Canal. Servants remarked that they looked happy with one another as, of course, was only to be expected.

17

Setting up a Practice
1455–56

icolò began his search for a suitable location for his practice. He knew, this being Venice, that patients would not go to a surgery in a poor area of the city. He must find a building on the Grand Canal, or at least near the Grand Canal, install state-of-the-art equipment and recruit well-turned-out staff to make the right impression per fare una bella figura, as the saying goes. He was fortunate in having Clara's dowry to help pay the considerable costs and he found a suite of rooms on the first floor of a palazzo fronting onto the Grand Canal near the Rialto with good access for patients from the

Grand Canal and from the piazza behind the house. He discussed it all with Clara because her family was providing the finance, and more importantly, he wanted her to be his equal partner in all their important decisions. It was all part of his vision for the role of men and women in this Renaissance age. In his view, the fall of Constantinople, looked at from a historic perspective, spelt the end of medieval superstition and ignorance. Like some aged duchess laden with jewels, it had been time for Byzantium to give way to the new order. Men and women would advance together into the new age with confidence and enthusiasm. Clara was not so sure that Venetian society was ready for such a radical transformation in the role of women and said so.

As far as the practice was concerned, Nicolò thought it fairer to charge high fees to wealthy clients but to treat poorer people at lower rates or free of charge. If he charged high fees to his rich patients, they would assume that he was a good doctor and that his advice was worth paying for and that their payments would help to subsidise the poorer patients as Christian duty required. He discussed the proposed fees with Clara who thought that her husband's approach was the right one. She agreed to help with the administration of the practice as much as possible.

However, Nicolò could dedicate only half of his time to the private practice because of his commitments to the military. It soon became clear that he could not do everything himself but would need another doctor to work with him. The obvious choice was Clara's brother, Angelo Foscari, who had studied with Nicolò at Padua. Angelo was a researcher at Padua University into the causes and frequency of outbreaks of the plague which regularly inflicted countries in the Middle East. Nicolò asked Angelo if he would consider joining the practice, and his reply was an enthusiastic 'Yes', so a partnership agreement was swiftly concluded. The two families felt that this was a good arrangement since any profits earned by the two would add to the overall family wealth and their complementary skills would benefit patients.

Angelo was the more outgoing of the partners and enjoyed marketing to the noble families around the city. He was an engaging young man, a bon vivant who enjoyed a good bottle of wine over dinner and was an amusing raconteur but also an excellent doctor. The partners signed the lease on the property and opened their doors to their first patients just three months later.

Disappointingly, that first morning, there was no queue of patients as there had been in Galata when Nicolò had opened his practice there. But Venice was a more sophisticated society with a number of private medical practitioners and hospitals run by monasteries. Inevitably, it took time to attract patients. Determined marketing of their services by Angelo, who personally visited families he knew, and by Clara, who worked hard to persuade her society friends to register their families with the practice, were successful. Even so, it took another year before they had enough patients to keep the two doctors busy and pay themselves modest salaries.

Advances in medicine included new chemical processes such as distillation and the use of alcohols to purify and identify the active elements in herbal remedies. These advances, researched at Padua University, permitted the development of more effective herbal medicines which the two partners were able to recommend to their patients. The importance of good hygiene was now better understood and they were able to convince patients that the use of clean bandages and natural ointments made of eggs, oil of roses and turpentine improved wound-healing in both domestic and military situations. Their reputations grew as the effectiveness of such new practices became obvious.

Nine months after the wedding, Clara gave birth to a daughter. The Franciscan nuns provided maternity care for Clara while Nicolò sat in his study trying to concentrate on writing up patient records. At ever shorter intervals, the sound of Clara's cries were loud enough to be heard in neighbouring houses and even in nearby squares so that most of Venice was aware of the impending arrival of a new citizen. After a final cry – a merciful silence, and one hour later, he was ushered into his wife's bedroom. The nuns had tidied up. Clara lay exhausted on the bed, pale and damp, but cradling her daughter in her arms. She held the child up. 'Here is our daughter, Nicolò.'

He took the child. How small and frail she was and how beautiful, with her damp black hair, and dark blue eyes! He was overwhelmed by a feeling of tenderness. He kissed his child, silently resolving to keep her safe from all harm. As a doctor, he knew only too well the dangers of infections and diseases which carried away so many children in their early years. He resolved to protect her to the very best of his ability.

Close relatives began to make an appearance – parents, brothers, sisters, uncles, aunts and friends. They came with gifts. The children rushed in clutching muslin bags of sugar almonds which they handed to Clara with some reluctance. Clara offered each child a sweet in return. The visitors congratulated the new parents on the arrival of their daughter. 'She's so like Clara,' the mother's family exclaimed. 'She's so like Nicolò,' proclaimed visitors from his side of the family; and all declared that she was beautiful!

The baby's christening took place three months later. Clara, Nicolò and the nurse bore the child across Piazza San Marco to the basilica. Their progress was slowed by the many well-wishers who insisted on seeing the baby and patting her cheek. The spring sun lent a joyful feeling to the procession so it was a noisy and cheerful crowd which finally reached the portico of the basilica where they joined other family, friends and godparents.

At noon, the great doors of San Marco swung open, the church bells rang out and everyone jostled and elbowed their way into the church and up the aisle. The interior was dark and it took time for eyes to adjust, but gradually the Byzantine mosaics appeared in the darkness lit by thin shafts of daylight slanting downwards from the windows in the dome. Every inch of the walls was decorated with biblical figures and pictures of religious stories. A gold-and-red all-pervasive glow of light wrapped itself around the procession like a warm and reassuring blanket of holiness.

A cardinal hurried out of the sacristy. He wore scarlet robes and a wide-brimmed hat and was accompanied by a line of priests and altar boys. Greeting the party, he led the way to the hexagonal baptismal font which stood to the right of the high altar. As they reached the font, Francesco Foscari, the Doge, entered the basilica to join the party. This honour he bestowed because Clara was his niece. The three godparents drew close around the child. They were Clara's brother Angelo, one of Clara's cousins and one of her married lady friends.

The ceremony did not take long. The cardinal made the sign of the cross on the child's forehead with the chrism of salvation. He asked what name was to be given to the child. Clara replied, 'Maria Clara Venetia Foscari-Barbaro', which seemed rather long for so tiny a child, but it had been settled by Clara, her mother and her mother-in-law. The cardinal sprinkled the congregation with holy water and gently immersed the child in the font. She cried furiously in protest, causing general laugher among those around the font. Clara dried her daughter with a towel brought along for the purpose. The crying stopped. Maria Clara Venetia Foscari-Barbaro was handed to the nurse for safekeeping. The service was over, subject only to the signing of the baptismal register and the payment of a suitably generous donation to the church. That completed, the party retraced its steps down the aisle and out into the sunshine. From there, they made their way to the reception which was held in the Barbaro family palazzo on the Grand Canal.

The Doge did not come to the reception, excusing himself on the grounds of work. However, before turning back to the ducal palace, he motioned to Nicolò that he wanted to speak to him. 'I should like to meet with you this week if possible. Certain matters have come up which you could assist me with if you have the time.'

Nicolò, sensible to the honour of being consulted by the Doge, was only too willing. A date and time were agreed.

When Nicolò arrived for the meeting, the Doge led him through a rear doorway and up a narrow staircase into a small room on the first floor of the palazzo ducale. He confided to Nicolò that in this room he could listen to debates in Council without members being aware of his presence. Over the years, the Doge had learned of many plots against himself.

The Doge came straight to the point: 'Dottore, you may have heard that my son, Jacopo, was exiled last year on trumped-up charges of bribery and corruption. Certain members of Council are using his alleged crimes as a way of forcing me from office. I am found guilty by association even though there is no evidence against Jacopo or myself. It is difficult to defend oneself against charges that have no factual basis. Perhaps more relevant to our discussion today is the fact that I am accused of failing to save Constantinople for Christendom. Council have established a committee of enquiry into the loss of the city, and I expect to be called to give evidence. You, too, may have to testify since you were in Constantinople at the time and were working there under my instruction.'

'How can they blame us for the loss of Constantinople when it was Council's decision not to send the fleet?' Nicolò protested.

The Doge smiled at the young man's naivety. 'The councillors do not care who is blamed provided they can damage me. On balance, I think it would be better if you were not in Venice to give evidence to their committee of enquiry. You have no experience of being cross-examined by a skilled prosecutor. Such lawyers can pressure even the innocent into saying things they regret later. So I want you to go to Corfu to inspect the medical facilities which is, in any case, a part of your job. While you are there, please get an update from Andrea Pizanis, who is a Venetian and the Grand Proveditor of Corfu, on Turkish advances since the fall of Constantinople. Find out how long the Emperor's brothers, the despots Thomas and Demetrius, can hold out against Mehmed. Prepare to sail to Corfu on the next convoy and tell your wife that you will be away for between three and six months.'

Nicolò left the meeting. He noticed how pale and unhealthy the Doge looked. The years had not been kind to him, and he was now eighty-three. Where would he find the strength to take on the baying hounds worrying at his heels? It struck Nicolò that he must be careful not to make enemies among the councillors. The present Doge was unlikely to last much longer and Nicolò must become, like it or not, more of a politician now that he was a married man with family interests to protect. He should establish better relations with certain powerful councillors and work to enhance his standing in Venetian society. Doge Foscari was probably right to suggest that he avoid the committee of enquiry into the loss of Constantinople. In any case, Corfu was a beautiful island and he would not be away for long.

18

The Conqueror Advances
1453–1456

 lara was unhappy that her husband had to go away, but the Doge was the Doge. You could not refuse his requests. In any case, it was only for three months. She suggested to her husband that he take Joshua Aslan with him. The young man was not a soldier like Bartoletti, but he was well educated and practical. Her father-in-law was willing to release Joshua from his job as his private secretary for three months.

Clara spoke to Joshua before they left. 'Joshua, look after my husband for me. Keep him out of trouble and bring him home as soon as possible. I need him here not in Corfu, and his baby daughter will miss him so much.'

Joshua promised to do his best. Secretly, he longed to find himself a wife like Clara. But he was a servant and Nicolò was an aristocrat. The young man knew he must look for a wife from a less exalted social strata, but he could not disguise the fact that he was more than a little in love with Clara himself which, of course, she realised.

Their convoy of five trading galleys sailed the following week. The winds were favourable and they suffered no pirate attacks along the Adriatic coast. Three weeks later, they dropped anchor below the castle in the Bay of Corfu. The Doge had given Nicolò a letter of introduction to Andrea Pizanis, the senior Venetian official in Corfu – the Grand Proveditor of the Sea. Joshua delivered the Doge's letter to the Proveditor's office when they landed. A meeting with Pizanis was set for the following day.

That evening, Nicolò and Joshua relaxed in the town of Old Corfu, pleased to escape the confines of life on board ship. They walked together down the main street which was a wide avenue lined with fine houses, very much in the Venetian style. The houses had imposing facades and porticos and were three or four storeys high. The local residents strolled in family groups along the avenue. The men were dressed in colourful loose robes so long that the hems stirred the dust in the road, and some of them wore Moorish turbans which added a touch of the exotic to their appearance. The women wore caftans of blue and ruby with long, open sleeves, and their heads were covered with bright silk scarves. They appeared to appreciate the admiring glances of the young men sitting at the roadside tables. Musicians sang and plucked their stringed musical instruments among the diners. It was a warm evening and everyone was enjoying themselves.

There was a delicious smell of fish and lamb roasting over charcoal, and the street vendors were doing a brisk trade. Joshua and Nicolò bought some grilled fish and freshly baked bread for their supper. Sitting on the rim of a fountain, they ate their simple meal as they watched Corfu society strolling along during the evening passeggiata. Droplets of water from the fountain cascaded around them, and tiny birds swooped low to catch the miniscule drops. Nicolò and Joshua agreed that Corfu was a most delightful place. After supper they retired to their quarters for an early night.

The dawn chorus woke Nicolò. Why were the birds so noisy and cheerful? He opened the window to get the full effect. What a wonderful day it was! He breathed in the crisp sea air. Birds dived in twos and threes over the roofs of the nearby houses, some settling on the pantile roofs, warming themselves in the morning sun. The birds took no notice of a goshawk hovering in the sky high above them. The hawk's black eyes were concentrated and malevolent. It was waiting for an opportunity to swoop and sink its talons and cruel beak into any bird foolish enough to stray from the flock. Nicolò watched, fascinated. He sensed the hawk's excitement at the prospect of a kill. Just as, he imagined, the crowd in a Roman amphitheatre waited expectantly for the Emperor's thumb to turn down to allow a gladiator to finish off his wounded opponent. Then Joshua called him to breakfast. He forgot the hawk and its prey. He was hungry.

They ate a healthy meal of goat's cheese, olives, tomatoes, eggs, bread and milk. They took breakfast in a leisurely manner, but it was still early when they finished their meal. Setting out for the meeting, they entered the castle at street level through a guarded gateway. They had to pass through three layers of city walls which interconnected with one another in a zigzag pattern. The hilly promontory on which the castle was built rose sharply and they were out of breath by the time they reached the top. The scenery was spectacular. They looked out over the harbour in which twenty or thirty ships lay at anchor, including their own convoy. Across the placid waters of the Bay of Corfu lay Epirus and a scattering of pine-covered islands. Beyond, the hills of mainland Greece were visible but partly hidden under low cloud.

Andrea Pizanis was waiting for them. He was a well-made man in his mid-thirties, tall, and dressed more like a sailor than a Venetian governor. In fact he had been a sea captain for many years and still liked to dress in an informal naval style. He had an open, weather-beaten face. Nicolò took an immediate liking to him.

Pizanis insisted on showing them the island before they got down to business. So, that first day, he escorted them around the castle, the town, the countryside, the vineyards, the river and the villages, insisting that he had set aside the whole day in honour of their visit, which was probably true for his duties were not onerous. There were some delightful parks and public buildings in the town. Further out, the villages were poor but picturesque with steep, winding, cobbled streets and small cottages set among dusty pine groves. Most people, they were told, preferred to live in the town for protection against raids by Turkish militia and pirate bands. Lookout posts were dotted around the coast as a protection, for, although Corfu was indeed a most pleasant island, even here one could not escape the harsh realities and insecurities of a violent and dangerous world.

The next day the promised meeting took place. Nicolò asked what advances the Sultan had made since the fall of Constantinople. What had Mehmed achieved?

Pizanis summarised the information he had received from captains of ships putting into Corfu: Mehmed's ambition was to take Constantinople. He had achieved this ambition when he was twenty-one. What would he do after such a success? Would he settle for the seductive life of the seraglio? Many diplomats were asking the same question. One former ambassador to the Ottoman court had visited Corfu and described Mehmed – 'The sovereign is well built, an expert in arms, of aspect more frightening than venerable, laughing seldom, full of circumspection, endowed with great generosity, obstinate in pursuing his plans, bold in all undertakings, as eager for fame as Alexander of Macedon. He burns with a desire to dominate. He declares that he will advance from East to West as, in former times, Western nations advanced into the Orient as if by divine right. Now Mehmed proclaims that there must be "One empire, one faith and one sovereignty in the world" led by himself.'

In my opinion,' said Pizanis, 'such a man will never settle for the quiet life. He wants to be the new Roman Emperor. I fear he will not be satisfied by the conquest of Constantinople but will want to extend his empire through the Balkans and beyond, even to Vienna and Rome. Bishop Piccolmini, the Pope's advisor shared this view: "Already the sword of the Turks hovers over our heads," he said. "Already the Black Sea is closed to us, already Wallachia is in their hands. Now they will invade Hungary and Germany." Indeed, the Sultan has not been idle,' Pizanis continued. 'After capturing Constantinople, Mehmed appointed Suleiman as city prefect to clean up the streets and repair the defensive walls. Suleiman organised teams of prisoners to repair the city walls to defend against any possible counter-attack by the Byzantines. Turkish officials were appointed to take over the administration in place of former Greeks. He ordered that Santa Sophia become a mosque with immediate effect and an imam now chants the Koran where once Christian services were held. However, in contrast the Sultan announced measures to encourage former residents to return and guaranteed freedom of worship for citizens of all faiths. He confirmed George Scholaris as Greek Orthodox Patriarch and attended his inauguration. He confirmed Moshe Capsal as Chief Rabbi and appointed him as a member of the Imperial Council. The Christians and Jews had the skills and expertise which the city badly needed so he encouraged them to remain. Mehmed took the same approach in Galata, allowing former residents three months to reclaim their family homes, and he signed a new trading agreement with Venice which gave Venice the right to appoint an ambassador to the Sublime Porte. The Sultan put his efforts, since taking the city, into measures to assist reconstruction and wealth creation.

Pizanis knew that Nicolò wanted news of the Galata medical practice. He suggested that Nicolò talk to the captain of a merchant ship recently arrived in Corfu, who might be able to throw some light on the situation. Nicolò went down to the docks the next day and sought out the captain. The master told Nicolò: 'The Turks occupied Galata the day after Constantinople fell. By coincidence, the captain had visited the hospital because one of his crew was a patient there. The hospital had been ransacked. Outside, in the street, were the bodies of patients dragged from their beds and killed. As for the staff, he had passed a line of prisoners chained together and being driven down towards the harbour. In all likelihood, they were on their way to the slave market.'

Nicolò asked, 'Was the hospital administrator one of them?'

The captain could not answer his question but thought it possible that she had been one of that dismal line. He asked Nicolò, 'Why did you not take her with you when you made your own escape?' Nicolò explained that there had been no time to find her, but he was not telling the whole truth. It was true that he and Bartoletti had retreated in confusion and run for their lives, but he had not made any effort to rescue Mary. He did not want to admit it, even to himself, but he had not searched for her, because his mother would have disapproved if Mary had come with him to Venice. He had assumed, conveniently, that she would take refuge with the Franciscan sisters. He had enough on his conscience without adding this latest news. He wanted to forget the whole dreadful business.

Pizanis explained that the late Emperor's brothers, the despots Thomas and Demetrius, had controlled the Peloponnese before the siege, but the Sultan sent Turahan and his two sons, Ahmed and Omer, with a large army to engage them and prevent them from helping Constantine. After the fall of Constantinople, the brothers resumed fighting each other. This fraternal in-fighting weakened their ability to keep the Turks at bay. Despot Thomas eventually fled to Corfu to avoid payment of the annual tribute to the Sultan. Despot Demetrius reached a settlement under which his daughter became Mehmed's wife, and, in return, he was granted lands in the Morea but had to pay an annual tribute.

'The Turks now control all the lands north of Constantinople,' Pizanis said, 'including the Morea, Thessaly and Thrace. In addition, the Ottomans have made gains in the Aegean where the islands of Imroz, Samothraki and Enez have become part of the Ottoman Empire.'

He continued, 'In 1455, two years after the fall of Constantinople, Mehmed invaded Serbia. He besieged the fortress of Novo Brdo, which lies between Kosovo and Morava. The siege lasted forty days, after which the castle surrendered. The Turks executed the city notables, three hundred and twenty young men were enrolled in the Janissaries, seven hundred women were gifted to the army to use as they pleased and the remaining population was moved to Constantinople to help repopulate the city. The loss of Serbia opened the Balkans to further Ottoman advances.'

Hungary was the next in line, Pizanis told them. 'Mehmed attacked Hungary the following year, 1456, with an army of one hundred and fifty thousand fully equipped men. Mehmed is reported as saying, "Once Belgrade is in my hands, Hungary will be subjected in two months and I can eat my dinner quietly in Buda." The Turkish army and its two hundred river boats reached Belgrade in mid-June 1456. John Hunyadi, the leader of the Hungarian resistance, could muster only sixty thousand men of poor quality and he had forty barges on the river. However, despite their numerical disadvantage, the Hungarian barges succeeded in breaking the chains holding the Turkish boats in the river and scattered the Turkish fleet. The Hungarian troops then joined forces with the defenders within the fortress and, with a force of eight thousand men, routed the Turks. By this action the Hungarians raised the siege of Belgrade and inflicted a humiliating defeat on Mehmed and the Ottoman army. As you can imagine, news of the Turkish defeat was the cause for much celebration in western capitals and was a major setback for the Sultan. Unfortunately, John

Hunyadi died shortly after his momentous victory. The Turkish advance through the Balkans has been delayed not stopped for ever. The despot Thomas took refuge in Corfu in 1456 but did not intend to stay in Corfu. He soon moved on to Italy and joined the Byzantine refugees in Ancona, continuing to plot and dream of recapturing Constantinople.'

Nicolò thanked Pizanis for his comprehensive report. He was now in a position to update the Doge as he had requested. They could return to Venice.

19

George Enters a Monastery
1457

homas the despot, Constantine's brother, told Nicolò that George Sphrantzes had accompanied him to Corfu. He explained that George had been unwell and had decided not to continue his service as a diplomat. In fact, George had decided to enter a monastery in Corfu.

George and Nicolò met for lunch in Old Corfu a few days later.

'Nicolò, I have a favour to ask. Would you sponsor me when I join the religious order?'

'I should be pleased to do so.'

George thanked him but went on to say, 'Nicolò, you remember my daughter Tamar? Of course you do – she was such a loving and clever girl. It grieves me to tell you that she died from the pestilence contracted while she was in the seraglio. My poor wife and I suffered such grief when we got the news. She was our youngest child and had a special place in our hearts. Helene holds me personally responsible for the deaths of both John and Tamar, and she is right, for we could have got the children away from Constantinople to stay with her parents in Chios but for my objections. Now she has left me and entered a convent in Corfu. She was brutally frank. She said, "I cannot bear to be with you any more, George. Whenever I see you, I think of the children and blame you that they are dead. It is too painful for me to be in the same room as you." Nicolò could think of nothing to say to console his friend.

A month later the friends walked together to the monastery. The ancient building included a beautiful Orthodox church and monastic buildings in the Byzantine style. The monks' cells opened onto the cloisters. Each cell was identical, with a narrow wooden bed, a cupboard for clothes, an icon on the wall above a prayer kneeler, and a small window. Silence was observed in the monastery at all times except for church services and at supper. The abbot suggested that the brothers would like George Sphrantzes to read from his history, *The Fall of the Byzantine Empire*, because George was such a distinguished writer. George agreed, rather enjoying being described as a "distinguished" writer. Presumably, in the monastery such residual traces of vanity would be rooted out under the watchful eye of his confessor.

The monks were expected to work in the garden or in the dispensary. They grew enough vegetables to make the monastery self-sufficient and herbs for medicinal purposes. The brothers provided parishioners with education and medical care as well as conducting regular church services. But the monastery garden was their pride and joy. Surrounded by a high stone wall to shelter it from the sea breezes, the garden was divided into areas for beekeeping, fruit trees, vegetables and herbs. Water flowed in channels along the paths. Every evening the brothers flooded the soil by removing wooden panels from the irrigation channels, allowing water to flow over the beds. They worked in silence, barefoot, with cassocks hitched up at the waist. At midday, a bell would ring and work stopped. The monks sank to their knees to recite the Angelus. Their lives were a cycle of work and prayer.

The abbot welcomed George with a strict injunction: 'Brother George, I must warn you that the life you seek in this monastery is not an escape from the world, but a place where you must confront your personal weaknesses and failures.'

He led them into a starkly functional reception room. The monk's robes which George would wear were waiting for him, neatly folded over the back of a wooden chair. The abbot and Nicolò left the room while George put on the brown habit. The abbot told him that his religious name was to be Brother Gregory and all the brothers would address him as Gregory from then onwards.

Midday Mass would begin in five minutes so the time had come for Nicolò to leave. He walked with Gregory down the garden path, under the shadows of the cypress trees, until he reached the monastery gate. One of the brothers opened the gate to let Nicolò out. There was just time for a brief embrace before the door closed and the bolt slid back into place. He found himself once more in the street and back in the world of men.

He could hear George's footsteps retracing the path through the garden to the chapel. Then the monastery bell rang to summon the brothers to Mass. When it stopped ringing the Mass had started, and he could picture Gregory sitting among the brothers on the hard benches under the white domed ceiling. It reminded Nicolò of the lunch at the Sphrantzes' house in Constantinople when they had sat on benches in the garden under the straggling vines talking of the future with optimism. That had been four years ago and so much had happened since then; but, in truth, nothing had worked out for the better.

Nicolò and Joshua spent the next month visiting medical facilities in Corfu. They exchanged contracts with a number of the religious communities, under which the monasteries agreed to reserve, in time of war, a number of beds for wounded soldiers and sailors. The standard contractual terms set out stipulations as to training, record-keeping, medicinal supplies and stock levels. Venice would pay a fee to monasteries based on the number of beds set aside. There would be regular inspections to ensure that standards were maintained. It took six months to conclude all these arrangements. Nicolò was worried that this work was taking much longer than he had expected, and he sorely missed Clara and his little daughter. They would be anxious about him, and he could not be sure that his letters had reached Venice since he had received no letters in reply.

Nicolò asked Joshua to book a passage back to Venice as soon as possible.

20

The Plague Ship
1457–58

he trading galley, *Santa Maria*, had left Trebizond a month earlier, heavy with swatches of silk, expensive cloth, sacks filled with exotic spices, innumerable objets d'art, uncut gemstones and exquisite Chinese ceramics bought from merchants along the Silk Road and in the souks of Samarkand, Kashgar and Bukhara. The Silk Road ran for many hundreds of miles from China and India through deserts, mountain ranges and the wide-open grasslands of the steppes until it reached the pleasant port of Trebizond on the Black Sea. In Trebizond the ship filled its hold with one hundred and fifty tons of these desirable objects, for which there would be a ready market and a large profit to be made when the ship reached Europe. Leaving Trebizond, the *Santa Maria*, with masts bowing under its twin lateen sails, set out bravely across the Black Sea, and down the Bosphorus, accompanied along the strait by shoals of swordfish and dolphins. Then it sailed through the Marmora into the Aegean, calling at Lemnos, Thessaloniki, Negroponte, Cerigo, Koroni and Methone until it had reached Corfu. After a few days in Corfu, it was expected to sail on to Ragusa and end its voyage in Venice. A passage home on the *Santa Maria* would suit Nicolò and Joshua nicely.

However, caution was needed. Nicolò had studied the recent research undertaken by the University of Padua, which linked the trading routes of the Silk Road to outbreaks of the bubonic plague. The study concluded that the city of Constantinople, for example, experienced outbreaks of the plague once every eleven years, and Venetian ports in the Aegean, including Corfu, were similar. The last outbreak in Corfu had been in 1450 just before the fall of the city to Mehmed. It was estimated that between twenty-five per cent and sixty per cent of the population of Constantinople and the Aegean had died from the plague in recent times with devastating consequences for individuals, their families and the economy. Transmission of the disease was very rapid. It was thought that trading vessels might be partly responsible, although how they carried the infection was not understood. Wealthier people tried to avoid the disease by fleeing into the countryside, and avoiding voyages on ships trading with the Far East.

As a precaution, ports such as Corfu refused to allow ships to dock if any of the crew or passengers showed signs of illness, and the ships and their crews were kept isolated by order of the health commissars. When the *Santa Maria* arrived in Corfu, a member of the crew was found to be suffering from breathing problems and chest pains. The man's condition was typical of someone suffering from pneumonia or from the pulmonary form of the plague. Symptoms of the pulmonary form of the plague were lung infections, chest pains, haemoptysis, intense thirst and lethargy. The symptoms of pneumonia and the pulmonary plague were very similar so the sailor's illness could be either disease. When the ship reached Corfu it was not allowed to dock in the town but was instructed to anchor off a small island in the Bay of Corfu. The port authorities downplayed the possibility of it being the plague to allay people's fears, given that Corfu had experienced the plague recently and people would be frightened if they were told that this awful disease had already returned. However, the sailor recovered after a few days and was released from hospital. The authorities assumed that his illness had not been the plague but pneumonia. The ship was allowed to move to an anchorage in the port. Here the *Santa Maria* loaded cargo and prepared for the final stage of its voyage to Venice.

The ship was due to leave for Venice in the next few days. Nicolò had to decide whether they should sail on the *Santa Maria* or wait for another ship free from any residual traces of pestilence.

Nicolò put it to Joshua: 'We have to decide whether to leave Corfu on the *Santa Maria* or to wait for another ship possibly in some weeks' time. What do you think?'

Joshua had no doubt that they should leave as soon as possible. He wanted to get home as, indeed, did Nicolò. The two agreed. Joshua booked them a passage on the *Santa Maria*. They said their farewells to Andrea Pizanis who was genuinely sorry that they were going, but they had done what the Doge required of them and now both yearned to get home.

A week later, as they were approaching the Port of Ragusa, the captain of the *Santa Maria*, Emilio Contradino, came to see Nicolò. 'Dottore,' he said, 'I have a sick man below. Can you come and have a look at him? He has a high temperature and is having difficulty breathing.'

The captain's words rang alarm bells. Perhaps the crew member in Corfu had actually had the plague after all. Nicolò hesitated but finally agreed to examine the man while taking precautions to protect himself. Putting on clothes which covered him from head to toe, including a scarf around his head, and gloves, he asked Joshua to fetch his medical bag from their cabin.

'Is this wise, master?' Joshua asked. 'You could catch the infection.'

'As a doctor, I have no choice, Joshua, but you should keep your distance.'

He took some scented sponges and herb balls from the medical chest and splashed vinegar liberally on his arms and hands to ward off any malignant fumes. He insisted that Joshua do the same, although Nicolò was far from convinced that these precautions would make much difference. The captain showed them to the crew's quarters. These were below the forward castle structure; they descended a short ladder into the dark space between decks. It was here that the one hundred and twenty members of the crew slept hugger-mugger among the cannon, powder kegs, shot and oars. The beams were so low that they had to crawl on hands and knees to where the man lay. The sailor was stretched out on a wooden bed propped up with dirty pillows and covered with a coarse sheet and red blanket. He was a pitiful sight, with his yellow emaciated legs. The patient was sweating heavily and breathing with difficulty. The smell was very unpleasant. Nicolò examined him for the bulbous growths of the lymph glands on his body. These swellings, often with a black centre, were a sure sign of the Black Plague and their presence was seen as a death sentence by patients. However, in this case, Nicolò could find no buboes on the man's upper thigh. If this man had the pestilence, it must be the pulmonary type which was just as dangerous. If that is what it was, the man could die by morning as his lungs filled with liquid during the night and stopped his breath.

'Heat a cloth,' Nicolò ordered the captain, 'and wrap the patient in it to let him sweat out the infection. After the sweating, dry him with linen cloths. I will return in the morning. If he gets worse during the night, call me immediately.'

He did get worse, dying as the sun rose out of the Adriatic in all its splendour. Nicolò ordered that the sailor's body be removed to the upper deck where he performed an autopsy which showed that the patient's lungs were bleached and lacked the redness of healthy organs. The autopsy pointed to serious lung disease which might well be the pulmonary form of the plague. The body must be removed as soon as possible to avoid the danger of spreading the disease to the rest of the crew. So, the man was buried at sea the same morning after a short religious service.

Nicolò stood on the deck. What was he to do? Should he remain on board? A boatman had moored his skiff alongside the *Santa Maria* for anyone who wished to go ashore and was prepared to pay the hefty premium to be landed out of sight of the health commissars. Nicolò realised that this might be his last chance to leave the ship before it was quarantined. It would take him just a few moments to cross to the deck and requisition the skiff. The captain followed his glance and read his thoughts. 'That's all right, dottore. Leave now while you have the chance. This is my ship and I can manage without your help.' The captain had a low opinion of doctors generally – in his experience they made extravagant claims as to the efficacy of their treatments, but many deserted their patients if they fell ill with infectious diseases and, in any case, most of their patients died. Nicolò hesitated. He remembered how he had failed so abjectly in Constantinople. This time the enemy was even more dangerous and deadly. There was no known cure for the plague. Self-preservation told him to flee as quickly as possible back to his wife and child, but he realised that he might infect Clara and the baby if he returned home. At that moment, Joshua arrived with the medical chest. They spent a few minutes checking the contents and the medicines. When Nicolò next looked round, the skiff had gone and with it his chance of escape. He felt a sense of relief that the decision had been taken from him. This time he would have to stand his ground.

The port authorities in Ragusa would not allow the ship to dock. They ordered it to sail on to Venice, saying that there were better facilities there for treating contagious diseases. The voyage took two days under lowering clouds and fitful winds. In those two days, two more of the crew fell sick. The captain reported this to the Venetian port authorities. At Murano, a medical team from the Venetian Commission of Health came on board. The commissars of health, after examining the sick men, ordered that the ship be quarantined in a remote part of the lagoon just off the village of Chioggia. The *Santa Maria* sailed on in full view of the city with its sounds of music carrying over the waters and the lights of streets and boats clearly visible and beckoning. In a gloomy remote part of the Lagoon they dropped anchor, the sails were furled, the oars stowed, the masts lowered and the *Santa Maria* settled motionless in the water within clear sight of Venice. The port authorities decreed that no one from the ship would be allowed to enter the city of Venice on pain of death.

It was distressing for both Nicolò and Joshua. They could see Venice just a mile or two away but were forbidden to leave the ship. The commissars could not tell them how long they would be held but made it clear that to get the quarantine lifted they would have to demonstrate that the crew and passengers were no longer infectious. In practice this meant that either the passengers had died, had recovered or had somehow escaped the infection. Nicolò estimated that it would take at least four months for the outbreak to run its course. His projections assumed a death rate of eighty-five per cent of patients who became infected, and that up to ninety per cent of those on board would catch the disease. The infection rate was very high because conditions were so cramped. It was clear enough that, at the end of the four months, very few of those now on the ship would be left alive which had to include himself and Joshua.

Nicolò met with the captain to discuss the best way forward. They agreed that they would not tell members of the crew that the illness was the plague because of the fear that the term "plague" engendered, but they would describe it as a pestilence of pneumonia and a chest infection. The sick would be treated on deck rather than in the cramped conditions of the crew quarters in the hope of slowing transmission rates. To further reduce transmission, the sick would be shipped after a couple of days to the lazaretto, an isolation hospital on one of the nearby islands where they would be treated with medicines supplied by religious communities. Life expectancy of those with the plague was expected to be no more than a week. Those dying on board or in the lazaretto would be picked up each day by the "monatti" appointed by the health commissars to dispose of the dead. The monatti had a bad reputation for corruption and theft; on occasion, they were rumoured to bury people alive to make their jobs easier. Corpses would be buried in mass graves on a nearby island. The stench from these pits could be smelled a mile away.

It was clear that a single doctor and one assistant could not manage so great a task so they agreed to ask the Capuchin friars in Venice for help. Late in the evening of the following day, two boats with lights in their bows approached the *Santa Maria* through the gloom. They looked like fishing boats with their lights, but as they came near, Nicolò recognised the brown habits of the Capuchin friars. The boats came alongside and the friars clambered on board. These men of God, some ten in number, knew the dangers and the short odds on surviving in close proximity to plague victims, but they came anyway. Their abbot had exhorted them to 'be ready to leave this mortal life rather than to abandon this our family and these our children'. They took over the day-to-day tending of the sick from the moment they arrived.

Nicolò wrote a note to Clara which he entrusted to one of the boatmen who had brought the Capuchins. He wrote to his wife in as positive a tone as he could in the circumstances. He did not tell her that their chances of survival were slim to negligible. She received his note the following evening, and her distress when she read it could easily be imagined for it was completely unexpected. She rushed to see her mother and they cried together, convinced that they would never see her husband

210

again. They stared out of a window, across the Grand Canal, over the roofs of the nearby churches and over the lagoon. There, far away, in the gloom of the approaching night, they could just make out the spars of a ship at anchor with a faint glow of the navigation lantern at its stern. It was only two miles away but might as well be the moon as far as Clara was concerned. That night she cried and prayed for her husband and their child until she fell asleep just as the dawn was breaking.

In the days that followed, on board the *Santa Maria*, things seemed a little less hopeless. Now they had a team of helpers, and they organised meetings early each morning deciding what needed to be done that day. The care of the sick by the Capuchins included washing patients, feeding them and cleaning up their mess. The friars wiped sweat from patients' brows and helped with the most personal of bodily functions. Most importantly, the friars talked to each patient with concern and kindness and coaxed them to drink medicinal potions and to eat food to keep up their strength. When the sick were in pain or fighting for breath, they held their hands and prayed with them. As they died, they administered the Last Rites and heard their confessions, so that they could make a good death reconciled to their Maker. The Capuchins did all they could to ease the path of the dying from this world to the next.

Nicolò concentrated on managing the sickness. He maintained a daily log of those falling sick, the number of deaths, the number taken to the lazaretto, and the names of those who were buried. Very few patients recovered, but those who did were asked to help with nursing the sick since they seemed to have acquired immunity against further infection. Again, no one understood how they had become immune, but studies showed that eventually waves of plague infections died out after two or three years so it was possible that the plague outbreaks ended because people had either died or had acquired some sort of immunity. In any case, recovered patients were not permitted to leave the ship until the commissioners of health declared it safe to come ashore. With each week that passed, the number of live patients reduced. The medical staff became better at diagnosing the early signs of the infection. It usually began with a high temperature and desperate thirst, at which point the victims were separated from fellow crew to avoid passing on the contagion. The facilities for proper distancing between patients were difficult to achieve given the limitations of space on board ship. For this reason, most of the sick, even in the early stages, were shipped to the lazaretto. The lazaretto consisted of a number of wretched hovels which had been built originally to house a leper colony. A number of the Capuchins transferred to the lazaretto to look after the patients who had been moved there.

The disease progressed quickly. Within two days, it would take a hold on its victim's lungs and squeeze the air out of them like a bellows before a furnace. The desperate struggle for breath was pitiful to see. In some cases there were also palpitations, spasms and delirium. In the final stage of the illness, patients waved their arms to and fro as they tried to catch a breath of air to sustain their lives for one more moment. As one recovered patient explained, he had felt like a drowning man trying to hold his breath under water. He thought he was drowning, but by the grace of God he fought his way to the surface once more.

There was no known cure. It was thought that the cause was to be found in the filthy air and noxious smells that emanated from crowded towns and alleys. To ward off the infection,

212

sweet-smelling nosegays were carried and vinegar sprinkled on arms, hands and other exposed areas of the body. There were also herbal remedies based on infusions of mint and thyme. Bloodletting was recommended. Nicolò was not persuaded that any of these remedies made much difference – certainly his records did not demonstrate their efficacy – but the medical staff had to be seen to be doing something to help their patients. One day, please God, the researchers at the university of Padua would find a cure.

Joshua and Nicolò both became infected – indeed, how could they avoid catching the disease? Joshua became ill in the eighth week of the quarantine. Nicolò went with the young man to the lazaretto, despite the risks, and there the poor boy lasted just a week. The Capuchins massaged his chest as his breathing became ever more laboured and did their best to ease Joshua's sufferings and prepare his spirit to make a good end. Nicolò held his hand as his soul fluttered uncertainly between life and death. The boy was so young. His life had scarcely begun. Nicolò was deeply depressed when Joshua died. The boy had cheerfully welcomed him home from Constantinople and over the months he had become a valued friend and travelling companion. The monatti came the following morning to carry away his body and throw it into the pit. The Capuchins said a brief prayer but not much more as even they were becoming inured to the relentless progress of the plague.

The next day Nicolò himself began to feel unwell. He had a high temperature and his skin was parchment dry. During the day he became thirsty with a thirst that no amount of water could satisfy. By nightfall, he knew for certain that he was infected. He despaired of ever seeing his wife, Clara, and daughter, Maria, again. He asked the Capuchin friars to pray with him for his recovery but could think of no good reason for God to spare him when so many better men had died. On the second day he was transferred to the lazaretto by boat, having been lowered down over the rails of the *Santa Maria* strapped to a stretcher. Once in the hut, he was laid alongside two other patients. One of them died the following night. He listened to the familiar desperate breathing of the dying man in the next bed and the murmured prayers of the brothers throughout the still night hours. He was conscious that he must make the same journey himself very soon. On the third day he endured the painful and terrifying experience of not being able to breathe. He felt as if he were suffocating and he knew that, without doubt, he was going to die and that this was the end. He felt the life going out of his body as different limbs and organs shut down. It was as if a lover had folded their arms around his chest and was squeezing him too hard. He cried for release. A friar watched his struggle with pity but detachment for he had nursed many in this state. He prayed for God's will to be done and that his patient might accept that his death was soon to be accomplished. During the the fourth night, Nicolò lapsed into a coma. His body was shutting down, no longer able to defend itself against the disease. The Capuchin waited patiently for him to stop breathing. He sat by Nicolò's bedside throughout that night, all the following day and into the next night. Nicolò clung to life against all the odds like a limpet on a rock washed by tidal waters. The abbot became impatient since he needed the friar to look after other patients. 'Well,' he said, 'if Dottore Barbaro refuses to die, you had better transfer him back to the *Santa Maria*. We need his bed here in the lazaretto.' The friars transferred Nicolò back to the ship. The monatti were disappointed that they were losing a fee for burying him.

By week eighteen there were no more deaths on the ship or in the lazaretto. The plague had done its worst. The commissars of health came to check the situation. They decided, after talking to the Capuchins, that it would be safe to declare the quarantine at an end after another two weeks. Survivors would be permitted to return to the city at the end of week twenty. The ship would then be burned, together with all its infected contents.

At the end of the twentieth week, the monatti boarded the *Santa Maria*. They put combustible materials soaked in pitch below decks, and placed small quantities of gunpowder up against the wooden walls of the hull. By midday all was prepared and they set fire to the ship. Like a Viking longboat carrying the body and regalia of a chieftain, the hulk burned all afternoon until, in the early evening, the powder exploded, tearing holes in its hull, and the ship sank as the survivors watched from a distance.

It was over. A naval cutter carried the handful of survivors across the lagoon to the naval dockyard in Venice, reaching the city as it was getting dark. On the dockside the commissars of health met the boat and checked each passenger for any sign of sickness, issuing them with a certificate of health and a signed permit allowing them to enter the city.

Despite these formalities and precautions, there was a crowd on the dock shouting and threatening both the commissars and the survivors, trying to stop them from landing because of fears that they might bring the plague into the city. Troops were on hand to quell what might have become a nasty confrontation. It was an ugly scene which showed human nature at its worst.

Clara knew the survivors were due. She stood on the dock wrapped in a long cloak to ward off the chill of the evening, accompanied by her father. They stood on their own a little distance from the landing stage. She had insisted on coming despite her father advising her to stay away, assuring her, 'If he comes, I will bring him to the house. There is a lot of ill will towards this ship. Some men think it would have been better for the navy to have sunk it with all hands before it reached Venice such is the fear of the plague.'

But Clara wrapped herself in her warm cloak and insisted on going with her father. It was nine months since Nicolò had left for Corfu. Clara had little hope that her husband was still alive. She had steeled herself against hope as if hope were a false god and not to be trusted. The soldiers opened a corridor to let the survivors pass from the boats into the city. The crowd shouted and one or two even spat at the survivors, shouting, 'Don't let them land. Take them to the lazaretto. They will kill us all!' The soldiers had to beat back the angry mob.

Clara could not see her husband. The line of the survivors made its way from the boats and headed for the city. There seemed to be no more passengers waiting to leave the boat. Then her father said, 'Look over there, Clara. That man might be Nicolò.'

A man, very weak and unsteady on his feet, was being helped off the boat by two of the friars. Clara was unsure. Surely that man could not be Nicolò for his face was drawn and his body stooped like that of an old man. Then the man raised his head, looking around as if expecting to see someone he knew. His gaze settled on her and he smiled as he always did when he saw his wife.

Clara called out to him, 'Nicolò, wait there.'

She pushed her way through the crowd. When she reached him, she stood looking at him unable to credit that he was still alive. Clara took his hands into her own. 'Thank God you are home, Nicolò. I had given up hope. Now I can look after you as I should. I will make you well again.'

'I always come back, you see, wife,' he said, 'like a bad penny.'

He lifted her hands to his lips and kissed them as if he were venerating a Byzantine icon. He felt her fingers warm and comforting within the gloves she was wearing. He breathed in the scent of this woman as if to clear his head of the lingering sicknesses and death of the plague ship. Then they turned and walked with her father along the dock towards the waiting gondola.

Later that evening, his mother and father talked. His mother was distressed by her son's dreadful appearance.

'It is much worse than when he returned from Constantinople.'

'Don't make too much of a fuss of him,' his father replied. 'He needs time to get over it, that's all. With rest, his health will improve and he will get back to his practice and normal life. He is alive, he is home again and that is what matters.' That was his father's cure for all problems – work and more work! And, of course, the gentle healing passage of time, spent with those you love and those who love you, would work its cure.

21

Moving Forward

T wo weeks later, Nicolò and his father stood at the first-floor window of their palazzo's grand salon, looking down over the Grand Canal. The light was so bright that they had to shield their eyes against the glare off the water, so they retreated into a shadier part of the room. Already, his father thought, Nicolò was looking a little better. How quickly the young recover! He felt older himself with each passing day and could no longer shake off ailments as easily as in days gone by. Neither Nicolò nor his father wanted to go over the recent distressing events. His father believed in the maxim, "Least said soonest mended", while Nicolò knew that his father could not really understand the suffering of those who had been trapped on the plague ship. He had not been there. He had not cleaned up the patients' messes or watched them die one by one. They stood there together lost in their own thoughts.

His father broke the silence. 'Did you know we have a new Doge? Foscari died six months ago after he had been dismissed by Council. His replacement is Piero Malpiero whom you should meet as soon as possible. I know Malpiero and I am sure he will give you helpful advice, but remember that he owes his position to those who brought down Foscari by innuendo and false testimony. You cannot trust such men.'

Nicolò met the new Doge a few days later. Doge Malpiero began by thanking Nicolò for his services on the *Santa Maria* and for his selfless actions which had helped to protect the people of Venice from the plague. He would ensure that the young doctor was honoured by the state in due course. Meanwhile, Malpiero suggested that Nicolò should return, when he felt well enough, to his medical practice which had been ably administered by his brother-in-law, Angelo, in his absence. The Doge asked him to continue in his role with the armed forces and told him that his draft recommendations for improving and expanding medical facilities had been accepted by the Council of Ten.

'There is no doubt the reserve medical facilities will be needed,' the Doge said. 'The Turkish fleet is growing rapidly and they are challenging our control of the seas in the Aegean and the Mediterranean. It is all part of the never-ending struggle between Islam and Christianity which I fear will not be resolved in my lifetime. Your services will be needed in the foreseeable future so I will confirm your appointment in a written contract. Personally,

I think we should have done more to support Constantine, but that is history. It showed a lack of resolution by Venice and other Western nations which the Ottoman Sultan is sure to exploit.'

Nicolò felt reassured by the end of the meeting that he still had a role to play. The change of Doge might actually work to his advantage. He walked back home across the Piazza San Marco with a lighter step, eager to let Clara know how things had gone.

Her husband's brush with death at the hands of the plague drew the couple closer, making them appreciate just how fragile was their hold on life. They lived in dangerous times, threatened on all sides by wars and diseases for which there was no respite and no cure. Of course their first duty was to keep their family out of harm's way, but it also forced them, particularly Nicolò, to think more carefully about his own future. He had unique experience in battlefield medicine and surgery and first-hand knowledge of treating plague victims. In discussions with Clara, it became clear that he should specialise in these two fields of medicine After all, the plague and war were the greatest scourges faced by people. Nicolò could not cure either, but he could help to alleviate the worst effects by applying his medical knowledge. Meanwhile, Angelo would continue his research into the causes of the plague and continue with the general practice at which he was so successful. The practice grew over the years into a most successful and profitable venture and both men earned recognition and honour for their work.

Nicolò and Clara's daughter, Maria, was their pride and joy. She was not yet three years old but had learned to smile, walk and talk. She was much attached to her papa. She quickly realised, as little girls do only too quickly, that her papa loved her and could be relied upon to indulge her every whim. Her parents engaged a nurse to help Clara to look after the little girl, but Nicolò and Clara spent more time with her than most parents did with their children. On Sunday mornings, it became a family ritual for the three of them to walk together after Mass from the Piazza San Marco to the Rialto Bridge. Maria walked between her parents, taking a firm grip on their hands and swinging with her feet off the ground. The three of them liked to stand on the highest curve of the Rialto Bridge, leaning over the wooden side and watching the gondolas passing below them. Sometimes, the centre of the bridge was raised to let ships with tall masts pass underneath, which greatly excited the little girl. The gondolas, on Sundays, had elegant wooden structures covered in silk cloth under which fashionable ladies sheltered from the blaze of the mid-morning sun. The gondoliers, amateur or professional, propelled their craft by leaning forwards and backwards with elegant movements of their bodies against the long wooden poles. Crowds strolled on the paths bordering both sides of the canal talking and laughing. There were wealthy Venetians on first-floor balconies enjoying the Sunday morning fiesta with their families and wealthy friends. It was a colourful, cosmopolitan and cheerful scene. These Sunday morning excursions became a favourite time for their family.

After a year or two, they agreed with Angelo, who was now married, that the two families should buy a farm in the countryside near Padua. It was in the hills surrounded by vineyards – the light soil produced the white wine of the Veneto region. The farm was rustic and simple and they employed a farmer to look after it. The families used it for holidays during the summer. They dined al fresco under the ripening grapes on warm evenings.

The farm also served as a retreat from the city at times of the pestilence which visited the region at regular intervals. At the first signs of the plague, their families took refuge at the farm away from the city. During such times, Nicolò and Angelo visited Venice as little as possible. They saw a limited number of patients and insisted on strict hygiene and cleanliness for all who wished to visit the surgery. Venice became a desolate and frightening place. Each morning, as they walked to the surgery, they saw fresh bodies piled in the streets for the monatti to pick up. People hurried past without talking, averting their eyes while covering their mouths with nosegays to avoid breathing the contagious air. Inhabitants began to despair that the sickness would pass and life would return to normal, but after a year or two such contagions seemed to lose their strength and eventually faded away.

It was such a relief to get back to the farm and find their families free from sickness.

Some years later, Mehmed the Conqueror died. In his later years, he had continued to expand the Ottoman Empire through the Balkans and dispatched raiding parties into Italy, including Apulia and Naples. His armies occupied Friuli and Carinthia, which was getting dangerously close to Venice. However, reports suggested that he was increasingly in poor health. He had become obese and suffered greatly from gout. In the spring of 1481, he assembled an army for yet another war. On the twenty-fifth of April 1481, Mehmed crossed the Bosphorus and began the long march to Konya. Four days into the journey, Mehmed suffered intense stomach pains, perhaps from poison. On the third of May, Sultan Mehmed died, aged forty-nine. His son Beyazit succeeded him as Sultan. Nicolò heard the news of Mehmed's death without regret.

George Sphrantzes died in 1477 at a monastery in Corfu, aged seventy. He had lived for twenty-four years after the fall of

Constantinople. His history, *The Fall of the Byzantine Empire*, is recognised as an important chronicle for those studying the final years of the Byzantine Empire, in which he had played an important role. His wife, Helen, had died five years earlier.

Afterword

Farewell to Istanbul
April 1966

My new wife, Bridget, and I shut the door to our flat for the last time. We descended the marble steps into the entrance lobby and pushed open the door to the street. We struggled up the sharp cobbled incline with our suitcases to the taxi rank. The ancient taxi bounced over the potholed roads of Cihangir until we reached the Galatasaray Hamam and turned left onto the Istiklal and passed the British Consulate. A week earlier, the consul general, with his usual charming old-world courtesy, had invited us to the consulate for a farewell lunch. Now the cab took us past the squash court and the Pera Palace Hotel and down to the Galata Bridge. The bridge was lined with fisherman.

Galata Bridge was crowded, as always, with Anatolian migrants in dark suits and flat caps, carrying great bundles on their heads, hefting and working themselves into an early grave. It had become so familiar – the sights, the smells, the sounds of the street vendors, the chai sellers offering hot tea in curved glasses with a lump of sugar and a cinnamon pastry. I recalled suppers with my friends Jeremy and Harry in the floating restaurants below the Galata Bridge.

But now it was time to move on. The taxi crossed the bridge and dropped us at the entrance of Sirkeci Station. We had booked a first-class ticket, seats only, for London on the Orient Express. I hasten to explain that this train bore no relation to the luxurious, self-indulgent Orient Express that nowadays carries the well-heeled from London to Venice. There were no uniformed conductors ushering passengers to their seats with a glass of champagne. Then, there was only a buffet car serving teas and coffees, but only as far as Edirne on the Turkish border. After that we had to buy food from vendors on station platforms. Not only that, but the toilets were cleaned only up to Edirne and after that they became blocked and smelt appalling. We shared the compartment with a middle-aged Armenian woman who ate salted fish and complained if I opened the window even a crack to let out the smell. 'C'est froid, c'est froid,' she muttered, making sure we heard.

Our train pulled slowly out of Sirkeci Station as if in no rush to leave Turkey and cross the Balkans or anywhere else for that matter. The muezzin called the faithful from the Sultan Ahmet minaret half-hidden among blocks of dilapidated flats which lined the tracks. The train made its way past the ancient Byzantine city walls, the Roman aqueduct and the terraces of the

Topkapi Palace, whistling as we pulled out of the station to warn people to keep off the tracks. The wheels of the train screeched, steel on steel, as we rounded the bend to head along the Marmora past Yeşilköy Airport.

The previous night we had given a farewell party for our friends. The guests arrived. The music was turned up to maximum volume, the dancing was to Elvis Presley and the Beatles. Most guests brought food and drink with them. Our landlady, who lived below, made no complaint but I am sure thanked God when people finally began to leave about two in the morning.

Most of those friends we were never to see again. We went our separate ways. Istanbul was like that, full of itinerants. It is the sort of place you dipped into for a few summer days on the Princes' Islands, and winters skiing and climbing on Mount Uludağ. But once you've lived in Istanbul, everywhere else seems flat and uninteresting.

Bill Matthews
October 2020

Bibliography

Homer. *The Odyssey*, translated by Robert Fagles, Penguin, 1996.

Ernie Bradford. *The Great Betrayal*, Open Road Integrated Media, 2014.

Evliya Çelebi. *An Ottoman Traveller: Selection from the Book of Travels of Evliya Çelebi*, translation and commentary by Robert Dankoff and Sooyong Kim, Eland, 2011.

Roger Crowley. *Constantinople: The Last Great Siege, 1453*, Faber and Faber, 2005.

Steven Runciman. *The Fall of Constantinople 1453*, Cambridge University Press, 1965.

Noel Barber. *Lords of the Golden Horn*, Macmillan, 1973.

Ogier de Busbecq. *Turkish Letters*, Eland, 2001.

Franz Babinger. *Mehmed the Conqueror and His Time*, Princeton University Press, 1978.

George Sphrantzes (1401–77). *The Fall of the Byzantine Empire*, Massachusetts Press, 1980.

Nicolò Barbaro. *Giornale dell'Assedio Di Constantinopoli 1453/Diary of the Siege of Constantinople 1453*, Exposition Press, 1969.

'History of the Byzantine Empire 2018 and the Fall of Constantinople', Wikipedia (last modified 28 Nov. 2020) http://en.wikipedia.org

'Wound Man', Wikipedia (last modified 13 Nov. 2020) http://en.wikipedia.org

'Black Death' Wikipedia (last modified 26 Nov. 2020) http://en.wikipedia.org

'How to (and How Not to) Get Married in Sixteenth-Century Venice from the Diaries of Marin Sanudo', *Renaissance Quarterly*, Sep 2000, 52 (1):43.

Google downloads: amputation, impalement, medieval medicine, surgical instruments, battlefield medicine, Padua University medical research, the Arsenale and shipbuilding in Venice, history of cannon, gunpowder artillery in the Middle Ages etc

Bettany Hughes. *Istanbul*, Weidenfeld & Nicolson, 2017.

Map collections, Cambridge University Library.

Liked this book?

Please leave a review on Goodreads